B E A T R I C E

C
H
A
N
C
Y

BEATRICE CHANCY

George Elliott Clarke

POLESTAR
BOOK PUBLISHERS

Polestar Book Publishers acknowledges the ongoing financial support of The Canada
Council; the British Columbia Ministry of Small Business, Tourism and Culture
throught the BC Arts Council; and the Government of Canada through the Book
Publishing Industry Development Program (BPIDP) and the Multicultural programs
of the Department of Canadian Heritage.

Strophes and scenes from this passional first debuted in *New Maritimes*, *The Nashwaak
Review*, *New Brunswick Reader Magazine*, *Kola*, *Poetry Canada Review*, *left history*,
Graffito, *Possibilitiis*, *This Magazine*, and *West Coast Line*. One song was anthologized
in *Soulfires* (Penguin, 1996). The author proffers many, many thanks to the editors.

Cover and interior photographs: Ricardo Scipio
Italian map of Nova Scotia: Hines Museum, Liverpool, N.S.

CANADIAN CATALOGUING IN PUBLICATION DATA

Clarke, George Elliott, 1960–
    Beatrice Chancy

    A play.
    ISBN 1-896095-94-1

    I. Title.
    PS8555.L3748B42   1999   C812'.54   C99-910217-6
    PR9199.3.C5265B42   1999

LIBRARY OF CONGRESS CATALOGUE NUMBER: 99-61831

Blesséd Reader

Every line is true, or it is a lie:
Honey poured — honest — over lye.

*Ogni riferimento a fatti e persone è del tutto casuale e le vicende,
Personaggi ed i loro nomi sono immaginari.*

Polestar Book Publishers
P.O. Box 5238, Station B, Victoria, British Columbia   Canada   V8R 6N4
http://mypage.direct.ca/p/polestar/

In the United States:
Polestar Book Publishers   P.O. Box 468, Custer, WA   USA   98240-0468

5   4   3   2
Printed and bound in Canada

Canada

À MARIE-JOSÈPHE ANGÉLIQUE

ET LYDIA JACKSON

Non v'è più bellezza, se non nella lotta.

— MARINETTI

Men write history; Women are history.

— BEST

ON SLAVERY IN NOVA SCOTIA

They did ... trust in freedom's light.

— P L A T O

A mass ignorance exists about the conduct of slavery in the British North American colonies — including ceded Québec — that remained loyal to Britain during and following the great Anglo-American civil war that birthed both the United States and — a few generations later — Canada. Essentially, African slavery was a hemisphere-long practice, from Québec to Argentina, and the American Revolution marked only a minor disruption. Nevertheless, it is true that slavery in Eastern Canada (including Ontario) was a miniscule economic activity in comparison with the far more lucrative enterprise in the southern states of the fledgling Republic. In the northern, Royalist colonies, slavery was small-scale, a matter of household "servants" or of a few coerced field hands.

Stubbornly, though, slavery is slavery, and the black slaves in what is now Canada felt every bit as oppressed as their cousins in the United States, the Caribbean and South America. Moreover, slavery remained legal in British North America until it was finally abolished throughout the British Empire in 1834.

In Nova Scotia, where slavery had prospered under both the French regime and that of the Acadien-displacing New England Planters, the Macabre Institution was dealt an early, *de facto* death blow, thanks to the influx of three thousand Black Loyalists in 1783. The presence of a large body of free blacks in the province ensured that runaway slaves would enjoy some shelter from pursuers. Furthermore, the courts began to prove reluctant to return fugitives to their former masters. By 1801, slavery had become a practice that Nova Scotian authorities — including Loyalist Governor Sir John Wentworth — were hesitant to defend. Even so, slaves in the colony could be — and were — beaten, raped and murdered, and masters — especially in the lush Annapolis Valley — continued to insist jealously upon their "rights."

Beatrice Chancy is not a work of history but of imagination. It is not a polemic, but neither is it passionless. For, being a Nova Scotian of African-American origins (i.e. an Africadian), I will never know the furthest origins of my African heritage. I do know that it was disrupted by a ship and ruptured by chains.

— George Elliott Clarke
Durham, North Carolina,
& Montréal, Québec
Nisan MCMXCIX

CHARGE

The abolition of slavery ... is emphatically the duty and privilege of women.

— B O U R N E

La femme a le droit de monter sur l'échafaud; elle doit avoir également celui de monter à la tribune.

— G O U G E S

Dramatis Personae

Beatrice Chancy, *a martyr-liberator*
Francis Chancy, *an inquisitor*
Luſtra Chancy, *a sorrow*
Rev. Ezra Love Peacock, *an undertaker*
Fr. Ezra Moses, *an enslaved believer*
Lead, *an oneiric slave*
Deal, *a heroic slave*
Dice, *an overseer*
Dumas, *a seer*
Sir John Wentworth, *Governor of Nova Scotia*
Hangman, *a poet*

Chorus: Slaves/Liberateds, Planters, Soldiers

*Scene: This drama harries Clemence County, Acadia, an oasis of
nullification. Translated there as the chattel of Saxon-American
Supplanters, African-American slaves pray and expire in the
shadows of sunflowers, in 41 George III, our Common Era, this
nineteenth sour century. Their cries must shake the ſtarry floor of
Heaven.*

ACT I: *AMBIVALENCES*

*The old enslavement was to nature, and the new one
is of one individual to another, beginning with chattel
slavery and proceeding to the modern kind, where
enslavement has assumed the most grotesque form—
not only wage-slavery, but also bondage to the finan-
cial institutions which, in the present period, hold the
entire world in their grasp.*

— BAINS

SCENE I

*A plantation in the Annapolis Valley of Nova Scotia—Loyalist
America's strange, oriental peninsula. Nisan—fresh, rural Nisan
—after snow-procured rain. April 1, 1801. Apple trees blaze with
blossoms. Sunning itself between the North Mountain and South
Mountain ranges, five o'clock light lounges, one-quarter dark. A
coral-and-ivory mansion glimmers, its Grecian columns con-
fronting the succulent, disobedient wilderness near Paradise.*

*Enslaved Africans gather and circle counter-clockwise, leapshout-
ing ... They're prepared to cultivate orchards, to brighten earth
with petals—or petals of blood.*

Slaves: Massa Winter
Be dyin now—
Our icy chains
Will be no mo.
O sweet Jesus,
Won't we be free?
O King Jesus,
Slay slavery!

*Deal, 19, craves a gardener's Bible that she can plot into verses—
a Sierra Leone of flowers—daylily, lupine, bluepoppy. A new
Lydia Jackson, she yearns to tend sunflowers in a free state. Her
shoes are shamed through to blistered feet. She beautifies a single-
piece shift; a red bandana shrouds her corn-rowed hair. Her black-
ness, big-boned, colours liberty.*

Deal: (*Laughing*) Tonight, I'm gonna eat till I'm ashamed.

Lead, whose name is metal, fractures the circle. At 21, he is muscled, upset élégance, a chevalier with tufted speech. He dresses a brass earring, weary linen pants and a miserable shirt. He wants his bull-faced fist to smash air in black judgment.

Lead: Deal, what's we got to joy about?

Father Ezra Moses, 30, a summoned minister, refuses a debased faith, minted from tin and copper, that glints in the shadows of annihilation, and that yields not a jot of light to lead the lost onwards to revelation. He is wedded to an alderwood staff.

Moses: Almighty God who rents us breath.

Lead: Mose, He can take back mine right now:
    This life here ain't no life —
    We smile as they whip us,
    Grin as our weak flesh breaks.

Moses: Boy, you jaw like you know somethin God don't.

Deal: Lead, you dull, jus like the metal:
    You wanna rile liquor'd-up pistols?

Lead: Why we always makin God feel
    Downright crippled, spavined, pissed off and tired
    With grunted, mumbled, blue-gummed songs?
    I'm sick of words!
    If prayer could bust iron, we'd be free.

Moses: Careful, boy, the Devil be real as fire.

Deal: Lead's rum-rinsed brain be as spry as a snail's.

Lead: Shouldn't you be stalled in a whorehouse, Deal,
    Stuffin strawberries in your mouth?

Deal: All of Nova Scotia's a whorehouse, Lead.
   Wasn't your mama born right here?

Lead: You want me to beat the blood out of you?

Moses: You's both jus two ornery mules,
    Draggin in opp'site directions.

Deal: When you spies a cucumber, Lead,
    I knows you must be jealous.

Lead: Your poontang stinks like an orangutang's.

Deal: You's a fool, pissin your spirit into spirits.

Lead: If I take spiritual gulps of rum, so what?
    I drink like proud parliamentarians.

Moses: Do you magine drunkards laugh in Heaven?

Lead: Drink rum and more rum. There ain't no Heaven.

Deal: Your shirt's so soaked with rum, you could drink it.

Moses: It's too easy to tear each other to pieces.

Lead: Deal's big eyes, a big mouth, and a big ass,
    And she sticks her tongue up Massa's soiled ass.

Deal: (*Shrugging*) You talk good, always mashin up white
         folk,
    But you jus flap your dreamin gums.

Lead: Like Samson, I'll haul down temples on em,
    Tumble to fathoms a thousand fat tombs.

Moses: You want vengeance like a drunk wants liquor.

Deal: It's smarter to hide hatred neath kindness.

Lead: I'll feel their gizzards crushing neath my hands.

Deal: Your mouth be steel, but your heart's weak as rust.

Moses: Long as we janglin each other so,
    We jus gettin mo wound in chains,
    An ain't nevah findin the key.

Deal: Mose, you bleats like some give-a-damn postle.

*Enter Dumas, 25, a harlequin poet. He hates our modern epoch.
Too many of us destroy ourselves.*

Dumas: This world's distorted—like love
    When hate's mixed in.

Moses: Ma Lawd's gonna hurl down fire;
    Ummmmm, damned sinner, believe.
    Ma Lawd's gonna hail down flame,
    Pitch snow-face pharaoh's grief.

Dumas: A pine spits a stream of crows against wind;
    They beat their pitiful wings against wind:
    Threats of snow harshly carried out.

Lead: Dumas, why you always bray like pentecostals?

Deal: Too much thinkin, not enough — ah — lovin.

Moses: No, he be supplely subtle and sly.
    He grins at Massa, jigs when he fiddles.

Dumas: That's so Chancy won't wallop this bookish
    Negro. I'd sooner be comedic than
    Commoditied to Mississippi,
    Where whippings get doled out just like candy.

Moses: That's right: Play foolhardy, happy, banjo
    Negroes, then pick up knives, and cut and stab.

Lead: Why must we be pretend clowns cosseted
    By pigshit? Rip open white throats direct!

Moses: Old men are philosophers;
    Young men are ruthless.

Lead: Young men sharpen their swords on old men's words.

Deal: Too young for philosophy, too old for pity:
    I'm uppity.

Lead: You're from Upper Big Tracadie, that's all.

Dumas: I see a vision that taſtes of sugar.
    Signifying dusky sugar surges—
    Like brimming tides—to a black man's reft arms.

Deal: Dumas muſt be balladizin lil Bee—
    Honey-tint Beatrice, who's been gone three years
    To a Halifax convent to copy
    White ladies' ways, as Massa always dreamed.

Moses: Not him, but Luſtra, who's aĉted Bee's ma
    Since she saw die the girl's own Ethiope ma.

Deal: Her name was Mafa. Thefted from Guinea,
    She washed ashore when that slaver, *Fortune*,
    Splintered off Peggy's crushing Cove, sinking
    Three hundred Africans. Bought as bruised goods
    By Massa, next seven years his forced wife,
    She died when I was seven, Bee was four,
    And she was herself juſt twenty-one years.

Lead: Let me drink dark rum to darken my sight.
    This hiſtory's only good for anger.

Deal: Lustra fit that natchal queen to her grave.
Self-blamed, and barren, she grew up Beatrice as hers.

Moses: Chancy's to blame for all these hurts. He seized
Bee's ma for his concubine. Shunned, Lustra
Caused her to catch a heart-freezing fever.

Deal: Massa's the worst dog God ever stuffed with shit.

Lead: Cock and bitch are blameful and killable.
But don't lyric Beatrice, in case she's changed.
I feel quite shaky about her feelings.

Deal: If you shake a little, jus take a little rum.

Lead: Thirteen when sent off, she be sixteen now.
Maybe she's forgotten that she's a slave
Like all us be. What if her heart's frostbit?
What if she craves to bed down a white boy?

Moses: We been scratchin her letters on spruce bark —
Steadily, secretly — three dozen months.
If she'd changed, them love notes would sign our graves.

Deal: Bee's too much like her ma to do us crime.
She could talk a rock into tenderness.
Didn't she always dance through fields with us?

Dumas: A white-coloured slave can backstab easy,
But Beatrice be dusky plum — true damson —
Down to her soul. She be our own daughter.

Moses: She now returns, this evening, this crow spring,
   While shoots suck their first taste of air.

Dumas: Is it true that they lie, the poets,
   When they say it is good to love?

Lead: Why should I love, why should I love,
   When my heart's scraped by chains?

Deal: A warm, plump bed, that's all Love is.

Lead: Why does gold-tint Beatrice worry my soul?
   She be half that chalk that dirtied her ma.

Deal: You relish Bee, Lead, like thieves relish jewels.

Dumas: I see her hand, it is gilded honey.

Lead: I feel dented, indentured, damned.

*Enter Dice, a vitiligo'd Goliath, primped in a longcoat, ready to
drool orders out of a busted mouth. Fear is in his soul like a leeching
thing. His face is a shipwreck. On the mansion steps, he glowers —
exiled from compassion. He's 21, with a bullwhip.*

Dice: (*Aside*) Tomfoolin, lousy, hateful, black-face crows —
   You want liquor, but you'll get a lickin.
   Like God, like Chancy — my one pa, I whack
   Motherfucking bastards like snakes. I'll smash
   Your faces till you learn to love tears real good.
   Mercy from Heaven, there ain't none.

Dumas: Love gangrenes in blood-caked chains.
  Law butchers our eyes and hearts.

The North Atlantic ſtings black, New Scottish boulders.

Dice: Work! Work! Work! Work!

Moses: God ain't fled;
  No, He ain't fled
  To some yonder ſtar.

Dice: Work, or I'll whips you like I whips horses.

Moses: He's in the fields,
  Stooped low in the fields,
  Where us toilers are.

Deal: It hurts to push this hoe. Ma back's on fire.

Dice: I swear you'll friggin sweat befo you'll eat.
  Sweat, nigguhs, sweat!

Lead ditches his pitchfork. His eyes cut those of Dice.

Lead: What you mean, "nigguh"? You think you's snow
        white?

Deal: He's messed-up white trash with a muddy face.

Dice: Your face looks like horse meat thrown to a dog!

Deal: Leaſt I got a face, not a sewer-hole.

GEORGE ELLIOTT CLARKE

Moses: Stutter bullwhips on his unhearing ass.

Dumas: Disaster his hide; serve him misery.

Lead sneers into Dice's ominous, blighted face and sniffs the air around the thin, larval tyrant.

Lead: You's up Massa's ass so damn much,
   I can smell his shit right on you.

Dice: One day I'll laugh while lashin yous to death.

Lead snatches away Dice's curled-up whip.

Lead: You rat-eyed, dried-up, Jack-nasty-face,
   Pus-cock, piss-stained, strollin sack a filth!

Dice: I'll sow you sows of niggers with worms!

Lead: Talk what you want: Your mouth ain't good enough
   To lick the worms from your dead mama's crotch.

Deal: Slap the black right off him! It's what he wants.

Moses: His black is lacquered on — like plaque, cackish.

Dice: You're horse-faced whores, damnable as devils!

Dumas: That lick-spittle Judas, crush him in two.

Lead looses the whip. It vipers in the wind. Dice scratches up his pride.

Moses: Black like us, Dice, can't you back us?

Dice: I'd hatchet your skulls, sick your blood on weeds.

Lead: Watch it, boy: My skull's skimpy of patience.

Dice: The good that pinks my skin wells from the sap
  A white saint pumped into my ma's black thighs.
  You ain't good and you never will be good.

Deal: Dice ain't got the sense God gave a dog in a fit.

Dice exits. His curses eddy in the welling up of trumpets, a crisis of hooves. Iron wheels gnashing into dirt—past Burntwoodlands and the bluegrass Caribou Plains.

Dumas: Fools christened this place Paradise; I call it Hell.

Moses: Remember the Biblical Paradise.

Lead: I remembers a gold gal with violet hair.
  I remembers; her love shivers my veins.
  She is too beautiful for ugly things.

Deal: You forgets two centuries of whippings.

Dumas excites a banjo.

Dumas: Slow she came to the fields,
  Slow like August rain,
  Slow like forgotten song—
  Angélique, or … Évangéline …

April purls, breathless, in green branches.
Dusk accumulates blue in a corner.

Exit all.

↜

*Vaunted in a sable hunter's outfit, slashed black hose, a wine-black
silk vest, iridescent chamois boots, a broad, shadowing hat, and
a gilt-edged, grape-black cloak, Francis Chancy, 45, in full folio,
paces in his library, a warren of Sade, Machiavelli and deceit.
He removes the hat. Note his roach-like braggadocio. Dusk. Nisan
7, or April 1.*

Chancy: Buy a hogshead of stomach-stabbing rum,
    H. W. L.'s tragic Natchitoches tobacco,
    A puncheon of molasses, a keg of nails,
    One purebred *nègre* heifer and her calf
    (Pay £70 for the lot, not a *sou* more),
    And fifty-two yards of *Hobbes*-forged chains.

Dice: I'll hitch the milk-cows to the hackery,
    Journey to town directly and return.

Chancy: Dice, you must love me, for you won't run. Why?

Dice: Look, you's white — colour of God himself.
    That's what I like. Uh huh. When winter
    Drops, I loves to stand and let chill snow
    Coffin my skin. I shake, but feel

Born again, a real being then. Besides,
You've played the only father I've loved.

Chancy: Your complexion's like night-exhausted stars,
But go as if you could sue to be my son.

Exit Dice. Enter Rev. Ezra Love Peacock, 40. He stinks secretly of spit.

Chancy: You comical, wine-cheeked, horse-smelly priest!
Come, indulge the raw church of the senses;
Don't mount crusades, mount cat-eyed Negresses.

Peacock: I hope your cheap words don't forecast cheap wine.

Dressed in a torn, blue, chiné *lace tapestry with gold silk filigree accent, Deal enters, bearing a bottle of Marsala. She also sets out a pie stuffed with chopped doves.*

Deal: Massa, I brings you dove filet you love.

Chancy: Suavely, you satisfy my desires, Deal.

Deal: Massa, don't our true needs jus harmonize?

Deal exits. Chancy pours out wine and passes a goblet to Peacock.

Peacock: Must you garb your slave gals in temptation?

Chancy: Deal's a ginger-cake scullion — plump, slick, hot.
She loves me so good, I could just eat her.

Peacock: I shan't eat the chopped-up doves stuffed in that pastry.

Chancy: Your faith is just piecrust. It wants filling.

Chancy slices off two pieces of pie, handing one to Peacock, who takes a quick bite, then another.

Peacock: Aren't we just leeches swollen by slaves' blood?

Chancy: Ignore these agricultural niggers —
    Their blunt, rusty, ape-like faces.
    Drink up slavery's luxuries, Peacock.

Peacock: Chancy, I shouldn't toast their oppression.

Chancy: Slaves generate
    Coffee, chocolate,
    Apples, hemp, dyes,
    Opportunities:
    The Bishop's gold
    Is being mould.
    And cash is good
    To eat — like food.

Slavery is global industry and trade — the future.

Peacock: I look upon slavery as I do upon venom.
    I don't want to trample on Christ's body.

Chancy: Free nigrahs crimp in sick'ning caves
    And grub off salt and greens and muck.
    Survey my servants, plump as monks.

Yes, they break tools, steal, lie, and flee,
But they're dumb-faced, childish cattle
That need unflinching mastery.

Peacock: Chancy, the Bishop seeks
But the look of freedom. Free
Your slaves, then work them
At cheaper cost. Appearances
Are made to deceive.

Chancy: To be a man, Peacock, one must sometimes
Imitate some horrifying disease.

Peacock: Though benighted, foolish, errant,
Negroes are still God's loved children.

Chancy: What do you know of divine justice?
What is whiteness without blackness?
How can we be beautiful, free,
Virtuous, holy, pure, *chosen,*
If slaves be not our opposites?

Peacock: Slavery disputes and disgusts *Nature.*

Chancy: Ha! *Nature* is slavery. We're thorough slaves.
We hunger, thirst, sleep, wake, grey, palsy, die,
And have no vote in the business.
We are born, mewling, against our wills.

Peacock: Slavery shackles whites to blackest crimes.

Chancy: So does rum. So does love. So does the church.

(*Drinking*) This blackish wine cuts—ah!—like a razor.

Dumas enters. He begins to remove the pie.

Chancy: Jousting at chess, I won Dumas in New
  Orleans. He'd learned English in a whorehouse—
  Like some King George parrot. (*To Dumas*) Warble, Dumas.

Dumas jigs clownishly. His gesticulations mirror Chancy's gestures.

Dumas: (*Singing*) Grasshopper settin on a sweet p'tato vine,
  Sweet p'tato vine, sweet p'tato vine,
  Turkey gobbler snuck up right behin,
  Snapped im off a sweet p'tato vine.

Chancy: Our world's infected by slaves and poets!
  What tumultuous burlesque! Go, Dumas!

Dumas exits.

Peacock: Chance, you think violence is comedic.

Chancy: My power isn't violation, it's love.

Peacock: Do you want Beatrice to fear or love you?
  She is equally your daughter and your slave.

Chancy: I've sponsored her convent school for three years—
  An unusual blessing for a slave.
  But she's my daughter.

Peacock: As Dice is your son?

Chancy: It's speculated, but I've my dark doubts.
　　My son must be white and known to be white.

Peacock: Will Lustra deliver you such an heir?

Chancy: Her womb is desert; it denies my seed.
　　Excepting Beatrice, I'll have no offspring.

Peacock: Now that she's sixteen, you could sell Beatrice.

Chancy: She's too expensive to waste. I'll graft her
　　On some slavery-endorsing Tory
　　To fat my interests in the Assembly.

Peacock: Chancy, I would buy Beatrice, if you like.

Chancy: Oui, mon hypocrite lecher, *mon Salammbô, mon* friar!
　　You are chaste, I think, Peacock, as a whore.

Peacock: Ite, maledictic, in ignem eternum.

Chancy: The truth falls suicidal in your mouth.

Chancy exits. Peacock's speech is curled leaves rasping over gravel.

Peacock: I hate this diocese defiled by worshippers.
　　But I'll go, twixt April, singing, and May,
　　With sugar cocked, surging, in the maples,
　　With white blossoms caulking the orchards.

He finishes his glass of wine.

Lustra enters the garden. She glisters under the crow-imagined heavens. She bears the heavy, secret weight of what she knows is illicit love. At 30, she accepts that the genius of her culture is theft. She encounters Lead, Moses, Deal and Dumas. Still dusk, but lusher.

Dumas: (*Singing*) Nappy-headed Jesus bade
    Egypt's palms swoon to Mary.
    Pour coconut wine to sip,
    Let a bee dream she'll marry.

Lustra: Your slave capers license too much shouting,
    Too little faith.

Moses: Miss, the faith is in the shouting.

Laughter. Lustra shrugs, eyes Deal with distaste.

Lustra: Deal, can't you and these other chits
    Try decent clothes?

Deal: Give us decency, ma'am, and we'll wear it.

Lead: (*Aside*) Give us honour, else we take it.

Lustra: Quit nattering! At these words, leap!
    Lard, bulge, sag, our master's tables
    With spruce beer, hamhocks, johnnycake:
    Eloquent food chanting of love.

Deal: (*Aside*) We'll be as swift — as molasses.

Exit slaves.

Lustra: Beatrice, dark maid, now sallies home,
　　Thrusting through prickling, galling woods.

Hooves stutter into stillness. A musket blares among gooseberry and burrs.

Lustra: My husband's single child,
　　This coddled coloured girl
　　Sidles here like slow fire;
　　The precious coloured girl,
　　Sidles down like slow fire.
　　She flames home a woman.
　　Though I name her *daughter*,
　　Can she name me *mother*?
　　This word wounds and heals me:
　　I buried her mother
　　When Beatrice was a girl.
　　She comes home like slow fire.
　　She mirrors the woman
　　Who took my husband's love.

Dumas: (*Singing offstage*) *Beatrice is pure song,*
　　So elegantly spoken,
　　A philosophy shaken
　　Into a new language,
　　Demanding new lips
　　And a new heart,
　　To speak her for who she is.

Enter Beatrice, attended by Deal, from a dusk-sodden river mist. A lucent crucifix blesses her silk lace gown of pleached gold and silver. She bears a Bible and a jouissance — *of apple blossoms. Her pride is steel, unflinching, a material hostile to slavery. The Sargasso and the North Atlantic commandeer her sixteen-year-old veins. Her breath rises from pines. Deal exits.*

Beatrice: Paradise is once more my home, after
    Three lone years, stooping in cold, convent cells,
    Eyeing warships huddling in the harbour,
    Markets splitting mother and child. Always
    I longed to watch dark-passioned clouds sugar
    Snow and rain over the river. O second mother!

Beatrice kisses Lustra, passes her her gifts. Hand-tinted blond lilacs score this scene.

Lustra: Your Bible and blossoms will perfume our bedroom.
    And your speech is perfumed like a lady's.

Beatrice: I've missed the feel of rain and snow on my face,
    The gushing of melt-water through the creek.

Lustra: Romanticism betrays you, Beatrice:
    A mud-rain pitches on us, a black rain,
    A chill, drizzling rain, squalling dirty snow.
    Dante's Third Circle corrals our Paradise.

Beatrice: The heavy soft snow has broken down
    The forests, yes, but lingers,
    Impregnating the rivers.
            April succours such goods —

White witness of blossom
And lily-saturated rain ...
        Blossoms are their own seasoning,
Their own apocalypse.
They flower in themselves.
        Watch the clement rains commix—
The succulent cascades of rain—
And everything like that,
Things that *asolare* in *Aprile*,
Slurring snow into blossoms.

Lustra: Wolves yowl in bracken. Don't be poetical.

Beatrice: I know Mi'kmaq blood sugars, rouges, our apples.

Lustra: Must the book remember the tree?

Beatrice: Must the child honour the parent?

Lustra: Honour thy name, Beatrice, and live happy.

Beatrice: And forget my folk sweat day-long in fields?

Lustra: Why should you worry about slavery?

Beatrice: Nuns tore Exodus from our books; they feared
    Moses speaks satanic as Robespierre.
    Slavery bedevils and chains our Christ.

Lustra: Are you some coal-scuttle *négresse*,
    Stinking of lamp oil, tallow dips,
    Slumping, rum-sick, in a pig's sty?

Beatrice: Are you happy, Lustra? Are you?

Lustra: Happy or sad, what does it matter?
   What difference do clothes make
   If you're always naked underneath?

Beatrice: What?

Lustra: The innocent rotting of wood—
   That undetected, romantic decay—
   If only he'd mimic that ...
   Undamnable.

A damp, mushroom odour of shame, a whiff of disease, prowls among the flowers.

Lustra: (*Sighing*) But the same hand that fondles ... torn
         flowers ...
   Can hammer your mouth—so it hurts to speak.

Beatrice: I'm his daughter, your stepdaughter. Tell me!

Lustra: Often, I feel I'm no real wife,
   Just the queen slave of his harem.

Beatrice: Father?

Lustra: (*Nodding*) Civilization in wolf's shape.

Beatrice: Nobody is beyond redemption.

Lustra: But he lunges after sin, pursues it.

He sluices down to estuaries of lust,
Seizes pleasure (as he deems it)
From lush, wholesale, open females
Who are pretty, yes, but in an ugly way,
Whose only perfume is sweat of manure;
Later, to our bed, lugs their smell —
An aroma of saffron that hennas everything
So I can hardly breathe —
The moaning scents of coloured women —
Like pungent, burnt orange,
The heavy, smoked taste of despair.

Beatrice: Who can condemn these women for his lust?
(*Aside*) My mother was a martyr to his lust!

Lustra: Constituencies of love hemorrhage in the dark
Whenever he stains his steel in ... insects.

The slaves enter and encircle Beatrice, gather her home.

Slaves: (*Singing*) Are you standin in the midst of Israel?
Are you pressin on up yonders?

Beatrice: A spindly girl, wading dew-drizzled grass,
I plucked plump apples while you plucked plump songs.
My love is your ocean-longing glances
Under this violet-blue sky smelling of stars.

The aroma of her speech — music sheathed in cherries, a lilting.

Deal: You out-pretty Queen Charlotte Sophia.

Dumas: In nectar-like flesh, with uncorrupt love.

Beatrice: Each line of your faces be sun-inked song.

Celebration. Guns yatter, horns gabble, fangs redden. Trumpets squawk.

Lustra: Our lord slogs home from wolf-impounded woods.
   A suggestive parting of air.
   Dress jubilately, Beatrice, for our feast:
   Flaunt a fresh armistice of flowers.

Lustra exits. Beatrice, demure, smiles. Spontaneous cheers, whistles, whoops. An impolitic, impromptu party.

Dumas: Time to bend a fiddle
   And break that bow,
   Catch your love by the middle
   And swing er low.

Moses: Bee's so beautiful, she should feel ashamed!

Lead segues up to Beatrice.

Lead: Bee, you's balm for ma hurt eyes, sweet queen bee,
   When I see you, I bout melt to honey.

Dumas: She's honey looks wrapped in molasses silk.

Beatrice: Lead, your smile is still like warming copper.

Deal: Massa bes not sniff out this fond chatter.

Lead: If Massa don't know, Massa don't matter.

Deal: Bee, be careful about your daddy. Try
To put shame on him and drag him to church.

Beatrice: If true loves muſt part, everyone muſt part.

Moses: What's that scripture posed to figure?

Lead: Figure bout time you scat. We gotta chat.

Deal: Lead wants to talk and squash and grass with Bee.

Lead: Deal, don't you go and get ma dander up!

Deal: Jus don't go gettin anythin else up!

Beatrice: We can waft some prayers up — to buttress joy
And make this April 1ſt moſt beautiful.

Dumas: Who can speak of love and be sorrowful?

All exit save Beatrice and Lead.

Lead: Three years gone, you're so extra pretty now:
You used to be lovely as dew-wet plums,
Now you're beautiful as moonlit roses.

Beatrice: Quit your voluptuous foolishness, Lead!

Lead: Ain't we guaranteed to wed each other?

A shotgun blast of dry thunder.

Beatrice: What was that?

Lead: Nothin.

Beatrice: No, something —
  Frenzied horses.

Lead's arms adorn Beatrice; he sings in a whisper as they waltz …

Lead: Oh darling,
  Be mine soon.
  The starling
  In the moon
  Cries as strong
  As the sea:
  "Death is long,
  Love is free."

Beatrice: Leave me to pray awhile, to give thanks. Then …

Lead: (*Gesturing*) I'll be down by the plum river,
  Under mauve blossoms, jus yonder.

Exit Lead. Nearby, a gun peals. Daylight peels away. Water quarrels in its channels.

Beatrice: Oh Father, Who art in Heaven,
  Lead's steady love is a blessing.
  But may I steal one more blessing?
  Heal my father's sin-cankered soul.

Enter Peacock, caressing a Bible. He spies Beatrice and hunkers behind a hedge.

Peacock: (*Aside*) Is Beatrix Cincia sacred? No, no.
    Sin will stun her inlets—suave sepulchres—
    Inculpate her in precocious sweating;
    She'll batten on hardness like any whore.
    Black slave hussies are only born
    To nasty, baste, breed and suckle.

Beatrice pursues her suit.

Beatrice: God, steer my father from his practised sins,
    While April blanches, broods, in the fields.

Peacock rises in a whirlwind of ruined flowers.

Peacock: Beatrice Chancy, confess: Are you still chaste?

Beatrice: Sir Peacock! I'm as honest as your mother was.

Peacock: Don't you crave a peach with a worm in it?

Beatrice: Cut open my heart and see how I feel.

Lead redux, *ferrying a necklace of apple blossoms. He nears Beatrice and glares at Peacock, who ignores him. Now, moonlight slithers over leaves. A horse, Raven, hauls a skull-cart in the fields.*

Peacock: If some black imp essays to broach your lips?

Beatrice: Let him thrust home Christ's steel stricture:
   If thy eye damns thee, jab it out.

Peacock exits.

Lead: That gimcrack priest — that petalled dung.
   There's somethin he must crave.

Beatrice: Nothing he can have.

Lead: He look too mauger — like a hungry grave.

*Pure laughter. Lead garlands Beatrice with the necklace. Feel the
light press of his lips upon her indigo hair.*

Lead: Have you been good?

Beatrice: Better than your need to ask.

Lead: You remember what we was?

Beatrice: Rubies? Berries? Our love was like buried rubies.

Lead: Gal, I'm serious!

Beatrice: So am I.

Lead: Warn me now if our time be ruins ...

*Beatrice speaks in a honeysuckle, seawater voice. Love is lonely as
this man and this woman, loving each other alone.*

Beatrice: Lead, you had Moses quill me such letters,
    Such raw, hurting words and lines,
    Etching inkwater into spruce paper.
    I feared their ink was blood.
    I read them, hidden in the victuals you sent.
    Your words were second scripture, Lead.
    They flower in me.

Lead: I worried you'd prove big feelin, deny us.

A breeze of lustrous song pries tender green into poetry.

Beatrice: I grew up breathing salt water.
    How can I forget what I was born to?

Lead: Shucks, someone be ripe as blackberries
    And delicate as calico lace.
    Your skin's like roses sunk in cream,
    Milky as clear silk rained upon.
    This is what you be ...

Beatrice: Lead, you are the beautifullest man
    In Clemence County, a pure, portioned man;
    Your skin smoulders hickory and cedar.

Lead: When we were chilluns, your plum hair stroked
    Your brown shoulders, leaving sugar,
    Some tangled there from my fingers.
    Lemme taste it again.

Lead holds Beatrice's fingers against his lips. He dreams that rain will glaze her charcoal hair, her lips gashed gold vermilion, smother her chastely sealed being in untaintable liqueur ...

Beatrice: Remember how I'd rush to the woodlot
　　To pour you tea, watch you plummet down pines?

Lead: I caught you watchin power pump in my arms.
　　Five years your elder, I knew I'd not know
　　Joy less I could dam you up like water.
　　The three years you been gone, my heart's felt dry.

Beatrice: Am I still the only gal you adore?

Lead: I couldn't savour any straying kiss.

Beatrice: One night, I'll grin in a warm nest of grass
　　And clasp you with my lips partly parted and soft.

Lead: You look jus like a fig tastes:
　　May water, sugar tea, some long sweetness.

Beatrice: All our lives, we'll find each other
　　Finding each other beautiful.

Lead leaves Beatrice almost breathless. If she omits touching even one curl of his hair, the chain of stars will fall. Let these lovers have their complicated sweets.

Lead: Lovin you, I feel free. Can't stand no chains.
　　Let's slip to Newfoundland, to our freedom.

Beatrice: We're slaves, but we're Christians.

Lead: But we're slaves.

Beatrice: I came to Paradise, sagging through leaves,
    A landscape shaken with longing.
    I've only just come home.

Lead: Massa'll only wed us if my fists force him to.

Beatrice: No, no, tenderly, tenderly,
    I'll do the asking.
    Women are better at persuasion.

Lead: Why does the slave ever love?
    Hatred be so much simpler ...

Beatrice: Because God so loves us.

Lead's burnt umber muscularity dazes Beatrice. The two lovers jousting against stunning loneliness. Sudden uprising of dark music beneath brilliant petals. Then, some clouds.

Lead: My black woman,
                I run to you, not caring
        If the globe breaks up
                Under my feet.

Beatrice: (*Singing*) Then the tree spoke unto her
    And it began to bend,
    Singing, "Mary, gather apples
    From the uttermost limb,"

Singing, "Mary, gather apples
From the uttermost limb."

Lead: That song's suave as velvet, sable as dusk.

Beatrice: My mama used its pain to lull me.

Lead: (*Singing*) Black pearl.
   You're a dark
   Black pearl.
   Black strawberry,
   Succulent t' th' eye.

Beatrice: I want to be the song you insist upon,
   Unable to breathe without it.
   I'm restless for you, singing for you, and alone.

A violet bell bleeds in white wind. Wheat shoots green under lightning. A spindly pear tree braves a black sky.

*Ceux d'entre nous qui ne sont pas venus au monde,
armés d'ergots et de crocs, partent perdants dans
tous les combats.*

— CONDÉ

In her plush chambers, Lustra sits before a coiffeuse. *Nightfall of April 1.*

Lustra: When I wed Chancy, his hands shone: Pure milk
Glaced my skin, silk that whitens white.
The next dawn, I felt snow kissing upon
My face—white like our blessed love was white.

A knock. Peacock fidgets into the room.

Peacock: Chancy is breaching the front gates. Ramping.

Lustra: I wish he'd quit this slavery business:
We're just ripening cannibals.
Our white lives give sunlight no more.

Peacock: Slavery satisfies our ordained world
Where wolves and blossoms co-exist.

Lustra: Slavery is splitting husbands from wives.

Wolves wail in the fetid, musty distance.

Peacock: The issue's tender. Don't be cavalier.

Lustra: He's delving cavalierly in borrowed beds,
Delving in pursed thighs, tasting laced poisons.

Peacock: He studies sin, to medicine to it.

Lustra: Let him study love, and learn how to love.

Peacock: He loves Beatrice, his daughter, though she's black.

Lustra: If he can love me again, that's the proof of love.

Peacock: He loves you, but here, in Nova Scotia,
    Wives sleep with Bibles, husbands with whores.

Lustra: He peacocks about—prime, cocky, narrow.
    This is why I've learned to kill by smiling.

Peacock: Corset yourself, Lustra, for the banquet
    That trumpets Beatrice's honeyed ripeness.

Peacock exits.

Lustra: I remember how her mother
    Was claimed by Chancy as salvage.
    He imposed his lusts to the hilt,
    And galloped her through sin's wet slough.

    She whelped my love his article—
    Honey distilled from lye-sour love.
    How can prized sunlight continue?
    Is love still virtuous when cold?

A dining hall. Tended by slaves and shadowed by anxious candles and nervous torches, two planters — linen-and-silk-clothed termites — hover over tables of enough or too much.

Hangman: Busy with a dirty commerce,
   Chancy's sheets rustle like money.

Peacock: After they tire of war, his type always runs to vice.

Hangman: He's so greedy, he'd even steal the leaves off the
   trees.

Peacock: He's chancing his luck in bad rum, wrong beds,
   black thighs.

Hangman: Calm, blissful, and fucking without a care
   Harlots in the matrimonial bed.

Peacock: He makes unstable love in horse stables.

Hangman: No: He doesn't make love, he makes mistakes.
   His sluts have faces that are snatched from dogs.

Peacock: Poets are intolerant, wanting beauty.

Laughter. Attended by Lustra and Deal, Chancy descends a vertiginous staircase.

Hangman: Hurrah! Chancy! Bring on Chancy! A speech!

Peacock rears up briefly. Deal rejoins her slave sistren and brethren.

Peacock: While late snow fails, gangrenous, in fresh leaves,
　　The Bishop presses out blessings like wine.
　　Like Last Supper divines, let's vex the wine.
　　But first, Chancy, splay the gospel's pliant leaves.

Hangman: A parable, a fable, something French …

Peacock: Come, sing of stars that fall to tumbly seas.

Lustra: Or sing the riverbank fired by white stars.

Chancy: Stars burn out, flaming, in extinctless pain.
　　Water bays in beleaguered majesty.
　　Snow caves in on us, dusts our eyes and mouths;
　　The light congeals, then dies. Orchards shed tears
　　Despondent as orphans. Plays spawn treason,
　　Poems assassination. So raise hectic
　　Music, quake this night, crucify the wine!

Hangman: It isn't French wine, but it's very good.

Peacock: Vouch a different tack! (*Aside*) Vulturously.

Chancy: Brother Planters, late Loyalists,
　　Forget that waspish monk, Alline,
　　Who plagued our Anglican Valley,
　　Stinging forks and scythes to revolt.

Hangman: Let's dig up Alline's bones,
　　And feed them, bit by bit, to our dogs.

Chancy: If Methodists and Baptists flit,
      Vomiting black emancipation,
      Warn them, "We'll be damned if we do!"
      We'll dash and crush their wings.

Cheers and sombre, dying music.

Chancy: Taste Grand Pré wine,
      Annapolis sharp cheese,
      Windsor salt butter,
      Madeira Portuguese;
      Jamaican dark rum,
      Adam's rain-pale ale,
      Pickled melon, chicken,
      Cornbread, spiced pigtails;
      Oysters, fried scallops,
      Gaspereaux, and clams,
      Queen Eliza cake,
      Apples, sides-a-ham;
      Sour coffee, sweet cream,
      And chokecherry pie.
      A wicked kick of whisky,
      Newfie screech, or rye.

Moses (*Aside*) There should be more bending of the knees,
      Less bending of the elbows.

Chancy: Sup my wealth like crows taxing carrion.
      Guttle my gold. I've a fattening fortune …

Deal: (*Aside*) His gold? That's our stolen fruit!

Lead: (*Aside*) That's our wages!

Dumas: (*Aside*) We get religion, but white folks get rich.

Beatrice — a New World Oshun — descends the marble staircase. Once, she glances at the audience and lowers her eyes, lidding them briefly, erotically. Pearls chain her neck. Proclaimed by perfume, she arrives. An Anglo-Saxon reel unreels with a lilting, African twist.

Chancy: (*Clapping*) Make those fiddles quarrel,
    Fideles, like gulls, now that daylight's down
    And my daughter's come,
    Then break out
    Steps that stamp like rain
    Smashing on a window, sing
    With voices that sound like wine
    Pissing from a fat stomach,
    Or like the brook,
    Breathing like a Romeo;
    Jupe and swing and whoop!

As Beatrice joins and kisses Chancy, he showers her with flowers.

Beatrice: If I should miss Heaven when I perish,
    This gilt memory will be my Zion.

Chancy: My excellent joy! To hear the fiddlers
    Joust as my darling girl arrives; to be
    Excited by one, lulled by the other.

Beatrice: Tenderest love, father, I tender you.

Chancy: Spectators, I dispatched Beatrice to Halifax
　　To shape her more like us — white, modern, beautiful.

Lustra: Your daughter, *Béa*, comes home, our daughter.

Chancy: Behold my daughter, in whom I'm well-pleased.

Beatrice: Father, only your wife deserves such worship.

Hangman: Bea: A satisfying cut of Venus.

Peacock: C'est Vénus elle-même embellie par les grâces.

Lustra: We schooled Beatrice at my old nunnery.

Chancy: And so my daughter's chaste — like unstanched steel.

Beatrice: Father, hold such praise for proved saints alone.
　　Never grossly, unchastely, boast. Flesh melts.

Hangman: If a virgin, she's no Nova Scotian.

Chancy: Waters are famished for song she borrows,
　　While expiring men sink, caries-hearted,
　　Texture their moot curses with poetry,
　　Because they cannot savour such beauty.

Beatrice: Father, why don't we say, sprightly, a prayer?

Chancy: Dante's Beatrice, you'll hoist me to Heaven.

Beatrice: Father ...

Chancy: Regard: rare, Demerara skin—mare's skin.
   Look how she denominates her mother.

Lustra: (*Aside*) He celebrates that annulled cannibal.

~~*Hangman:* Slaves siphon the best blood of *Acadie.*~~ ⟨cut⟩

Beatrice: Father ...

Peacock: (*Quietly*) Chancy, your wife blanches with shame.

Chancy: (*Loudly*) It shames me this shameless minx is fallow.

Lustra: I pray God will unlock my womb.

Chancy: With what? A key? A knife?

Lustra: I'm not utterly barren. Here's Beatrice:
   I've loved her as if she were my own flesh.

Chancy: Who craves a dry, dull, empty, sonless wife?

Lustra: I feel faint.

Beatrice: A pious grace, let's say; a gracious prayer.

Chancy: Her throat flutes a sugared *citronella.*

Lustra: (*Aside*) My throat pipes hate, a knife harsh as acid.

Chancy: Purity tissued in unspecious silk,
   That's my daughter, of whom I'm rightly proud.

Hangman: She's immaculate: a sigh of roses.

Chancy: Less like roses, no, more like a woman.

Beatrice: All women spring from the same mother duſt.

Luſtra: (*Aside*) He bought her mother for a sack of potatoes.

Peacock: Chancy, Beatrice is hungry to be wed.
    Tonight, I saw her lover nourish her
    With appetizing, buttery kisses.

Chancy: What news is this? To couple so quickly?

Beatrice: Father, I dreamt of begging you later,
    Alone. Unpublic. I'm taken aback.

Chancy: I'm taken aback! This is swift error.

Beatrice: The nuns have tutored me to author love.

Hangman: Chancy, this dulcet news authors music!

Chancy: Who is your lover? Who is your lover?
    Who of my friends is my daughter's lover?

Beatrice: He's here, sir. He's—

Lead: Please, suh, we's beg you humbly the blessing
            to wed.
    We's both natural happy in our love.

Peacock: Hurrah! A toast, Chancy, a lyric toast!

An obnubilating hush.

Chancy: My daughter can't love some bull-thighed nigger!
    It's April 1st, but this is no glad joke.
    Confess, now, Beatrice, whom you really love!

Beatrice moves towards Lead; Lead stands forward.

Beatrice: *Poetry* in its most indulgent shape.
    To live without Lead would wither my life.

Chancy: And I considered you as my daughter,
    Not some slut, so low as to go lusting ...

Lustra: Husband!

Chancy: Mewling for the rough pawings of some ape,
    To coddle sooty sperm in your clean womb.

Beatrice: Father, you don't know what you are saying.

Chancy: You mock my love by loving dung!

Lustra: Francis!

Beatrice: Father, I love you as I'm supposed to!

Hangman: Peace, Chancy. She's yours to sell at market.
    That's stock I'll trade gold for. Where's my wallet?

Lustra: My only child's not for sale to your likes!

Beatrice: Father, would you barter me like a hog,
    Or wood, or a piece of machinery?

Chancy: You'll not buck, sweat, under a swinish black,
    Lavish moth kisses on a savage mouth.

Lead: (*To Moses*) I'll gut the skunk what pants against her
        flesh!

Beatrice: Father—

Peacock: The wine sits cool in the bottles.
    Let's not be disagreeable.

Beatrice: Father, you've drunk too much. Let's go—

Chancy: I'll cure that malicious mouth! Go!

*Chancy beckons towards the wings. Enter Dice. Night gushes in
violently.*

Chancy: (*To Dice*) Lock up this heated bitch, this mutiny.
    Let her chill—like new wine—in the basement.
    Since she craves a slave, teach her slavery.

Dice: Come soft with me, Beetrees. Don't play quarrelsome.

Beatrice: My sweet Lead, oh, won't anyone help us?

Chancy: *Bicé, Treasa,* you're nobody's slave but mine.

Lustra: Husband, I agree Beatrice shan't marry
   A slave. Let's not act like pirates, irate.

Lead: (*Aside*) They're both right-mean actors, suited for
         graves.

Chancy: (*To Dice*) Clap hobbling chains on Beatrice, but
            brand Lead:
   Show these lewd dogs how much we hate their lust.

Dice: Let em eat cowhide; they should be well wept.

Hangman: Chancy, why harm the things that make you money?

Chancy: I whipped a horse to death for eating flowers.
   I settle rabid animals easy as that.

Hangman: Auction Beatrice: She'd be exquisite, swinking in
            my bed.

Lustra: My lord, I beg you. Don't sell my daughter!

Chancy: You unslaked sore! I'll sell you, if I like.

Dice chains Lead and Beatrice together.

Deal: (*Aside*) Night of fire and lightning, night of liquor,
   Night of dogs, night of bleeding-mouthed laughter.

Moses: (*Aside*) Let the stars go black, let the world burn up.

Dice leads Lead and Beatrice out.

Lustra: I fear wolves are eating up this county.

Chancy strikes Lustra. Her mouth's a wet rose.

Hangman: Hitting her, Chance, is like hitting a child.

Chancy: After such blows, Lustra seems more lustrous.
   Wife, you will retire! Slaves, you are dismissed!

Exit Lustra, Hangman, and remaining slaves, save Dumas.

Peacock: Turbulent man, your deeds are wounds. Beware:
   Cruelty cannot be mother to *Love.*

Chancy: Our system is a machine of cruelty.

Darkness. The moon comes out and says nothing.

Dumas: (*Singing*) That awful day will surely come,
   The appointed hour makes haste,
   When I must stand before my Judge,
   And pass the solemn test.

༆

SCENE III

Chancy sips wine in his library. His biography: an encyclopedia of sin.

Chancy: Her return returns her mother's image,
   Drafting, in living oils, unfatherly,

Un-Christian scenes, for her lips conjure choice,
Delicious cherries, and God's Word glosses
Them like honey, but blisters mine like thorns.
Fresh from the convent and demanding love,
O Beatrice, dolce bella e cara,
You'll not amalgamate with animals.

Darkness. Closing of the First Day of Desire, or April 1.

᎐

SCENE IV

Deal, alone in her hut, glances in a shard of mirror. Thursday, April 2.

Deal: I'll run off one night of lightning closing down stars—
    Lightning white like death and cold like death.
    He hinder me, I slice open his eyes.

Enter Beatrice, bella, morbidezza. *She wears a soft white woollen gown, with gilt crepe quilling against her cinnamon face and neck, a blue velvet jacket, and a bandage on one cheek. The clock eyes midnight.*

Deal: Your creeping here dangers us both with pain:
    Massa lift you up from your basement cell
    Only cos you swore you'd never parley
    With Lead or any other slave again.
    If your pa learns you're here, we'll be tore up
    With whips, and I've sorrowed too much already.

Beatrice: Deal, you know something about love —
    What I hold for Lead — and nothing
    Unjust can legalize its hurt.
    Besides, you and I are almost
    Sisters: My mama nursed us both.

Deal: Under the orchard she lies, but she be
    Deathless. Righteous, your mama suckled me
    Till I was biggity. I give you that.
    So what you want, Beata, in your ma's name?

Beatrice: How's my love? How's Lead? Is he deeply hurt?

Deal: Would slavery be slavery if slaves wasn't hurt?

Beatrice: In vain, his lips, in vain, his dark-brown hands
    Called out to me, in vain. No pain like this.

Deal: Your face bears pain, but I been slashed deeper.

Beatrice: What is the answer? Is there no answer?

Deal: Massa's killin us as fast as he can.

Beatrice: It's not his punishment that galls, but loneliness.

Deal: Thought you learned about loneliness
    With all them nunnish white gals, Bee.

Beatrice: Am I supposed to be loveless because
    I'm schooled by nuns? Listen: tears wove my veil.

Deal: I'm just mooded for hate, too for wisdom:
   Steal away from here and steal you some love.
   Listen good to me: There's no other way.
   Can you make bread from shit or wine from piss?

Beatrice: I can't just confiscate myself, the law —

Deal: Slave law's like an old, warped, crotchety wine,
   And some old wine be bitter vinegar.

Beatrice: I seem solid, but I'm just thin ice.

Deal: You got the backbone to mate, or just the dream?

Beatrice: Maybe you forgets, Deal, how we once dashed,
   Crashing night-long beneath moth-pestered lamps,
   Laughter splashing hot like rum in our throats,
   Moonlight joshing gilt, delirious hay —
   How we turned and turned, heathenish in grass,
   And Lead joked I had a face like a horse,
   Then drawled that I was woeful beautiful,
   And we uprooted brash buttercups to suck,
   And Dice whined and whined for our strawberries,
   And we'd never give him a single taste.

Deal: Recollection ain't wisdom. What you want?

Beatrice: Beg Lead to edge tomorrow, Good Friday,
   Long the galingaled marsh. My heart craves him.

Deal: Lead's no apple-tree man with sand-brown eyes,
   No scars, no troubles, no lies, no regrets.

He feels nasty, and he looks nasty too.
Still, I'll pass your message, like a sistuh.
But if you get caught, don't breathe out my name:
I ain't takin no beatins cos of Lead.

Beatrice and Deal embrace. The sky is half fiery with moon-paled petals.

Beatrice: To heal the desert-hatred of this night,
  All I want is love and cool, sweet water.

Deal: Nothin tastes sweet when you're a slave.
  Take my wisdom, take Lead, and take off.
  Hive to the lumberwoods, hive out chillun.

Beatrice: Should I cross or double-cross my father?

Deal: Bee, listen up: A crooked place makes love go wrong.
  Massa plays Pharaoh. Can you play Moses?

Beatrice: I'll play Beatrice. I'll play her beautifully.

Beatrice, casual narcissus, fixes her looks in the broken scythe of mirror, while Deal watches, shaking her head. Then, Beatrice exits, smiling. Toll of midnight.

✎

SCENE V

A Düreresque light crouches over North Mountain, speculating on a storm. A graveyard backs a marish grove of pieced wildings and pines. Beatrice and Lead kiss while lying atop a weedy grave. Beatrice pulls up marguerites. It's Good Friday, April 3.

Lead: Doing that, ash-head folks says,
Uproots the souls of the dead.
So be rev'rent cos it be Good Friday.

Beatrice: I don't care. I don't care. Not now.
Love me fiercely. Kiss me. Fiercely.

The lovers' hands breathe benediction about their bodies. The river drowses among bulrushes.

Beatrice: (*Singing*) Two butterflies duet about my head,
Mistaking me for a flower.
Yet, I am a flower.

Lead: (*Singing*) The moon be iv'ry fire,
The winter's icy brawl.
I ain't got no mo desire —
If I can't have you at all.

Beatrice: (*Singing*) The night is tinted blue —
The windows frozen black.
If I must turn from you,
There'll be no turning back.

Lead: Your beauty makes this place horrify me.

Beatrice: If we should fail, if our love should fail,
Air will sour, rain spill dull, language fold,
Snow ruin, destroy, what's left of me.

Lead: We won't fail so long as we overpower—
    With Deal's help—mean hindrance to our wedding.

Kisses encore, but Lead sits up, losing a dream. He notes, in one saccade, *the sugar trees sicken. Why must love sweeten the cemetery?*

Beatrice: Who's buried here?

Lead: The name's failed from the tombstone.

The lovers loll upon the grave. When Beatrice touches Lead's chest, he grimaces, clutches her hand away.

Beatrice: What is it? What is it?

Lead: Nuttin, nuttin.

Beatrice: That's a lot of nothing for such a look.

Beatrice unbuttons Lead's shirt. She eyes a cruciform cut.

Beatrice: (*Gasping*) Wounded! I'm wounded seeing this
    wounding.

Lead: Massa branded me, but he's hurt you more.

Beatrice: Moi aussi, je suis blessée. Mes yeux saignent.

Lead: Bee, we gotta run. Scape to Halifax.

Beatrice: How? Can we run from one end of Nova
　　Scotia to the other? Hound-face scarecrows
　　With hounds will thresh roads and fields to snatch us.

Lead: I don't give a damn for any white son
　　Of a bitch — or their bitches. I'll kill em.

*Thunderclaps. Downcome. Lead and Beatrice stumble to shelter
under a lean-to, amid the* mocauque. *Churned rain rides in, holes
up, in terra-cotta earth, with hackmatack sighing in the mountains.
Let lovers wake, peck plums, and flee — like hummingbirds — to
dreams.*

Beatrice: Give me wine that can do no wrong.
　　Move, move your head from side to side,
　　Under my kiss, smearing our lips.

Lead: I'll dream always now of your brown-bark hands,
　　My hands swimmin in your wine-coloured hair.

*The lovers drift slowly into grass. Chaste bliss. Rain creaks in the
wind, spoils in the road.*

Beatrice: Now we're here, don't think
　　You smell perfume in my hair.
　　You smell apple blossoms.

*Sudden richness after thunder, the trees shaking down violent,
intransigent magnificence — the hours doused in perfume, the
lightning curling into the quick snap of eyes at flowers. As the lovers
complete their kiss, they are spied by Dice. He bears a musket.*

Dice: I smell your fishy flesh — or else your soul —
   Betrayal, and the nigger ſtink of Lead's own.
   I don't like your blood-smell, and I hate his.

*Dice fires over the heads of Lead and Beatrice. They scramble to
their feet.*

Dice: You's so drunk with evil, you sweats, piss, it.
   Go ſtumble from bramble to bramble,
   My shot'll uncover — like wildfire — your hides.

Dice herds Lead and Beatrice offſtage.

ACT III: *VICTIMS*

A mausoleum of white lucense in dark emptiness. The white, arctic darkness of primal sin. Gradually, this light — the cold beam of civil savagery — widens to reveal eels of chain writhing on stony walls. A bleak, jellied rancidness. Beatrice lies face up on a bed.

Beatrice: Pines crack like rigid blackgreen fire;
    I turn, and the moon's hard in my eyes,
    This nervous, dying April,
    A river smashing blind —
    Broken-winged bird —
    Into stone.

A door jars open. A candle soughs into life. Good Friday, burning low.

Chancy: How's my fool and russet romantic now?

Beatrice: Father, untie me, please. Please, I'm quite cold.

Chancy: Your skin's cold, your heart's cold, your eyes are
        cold —
    Darkly void of any loving feeling.

Beatrice: Where's my love? Where is Lead?

Chancy drags a finger across Beatrice's lips, driving them apart.

Chancy: Why do you let fecal lips soil these corals?

Beatrice wrenches her head away.

Chancy: Your paramour's being horsewhipped as we jest.

Beatrice: We love purely, you love purely to hate.

Chancy: Should I respect a thing got of a spasm?

Beatrice: Tenderly, I love you, as your daughter.

Chancy: Tender, you purr, mince, swish. Abhorrent whore!
   You're young, but so precociously lustful,
   Soliciting illicit kisses in mud.

Beatrice: I have been upright as guiltless lilies.

Chancy: But you lay down to play Cleopatra,
   To prostitute yourself in cow pastures.

Beatrice: I wasn't unbecoming, I wasn't compromised.

Chancy: You were fretted, shovelled, like so much dirt,
   Blasting thus my flowers and this Good Friday.

Beatrice: I strive always to buckle onto God.

Chancy: One night, you'll unbuckle a man's breeches.
   You'll pant and grunt and roach up sweating sheets.

Beatrice: I know how a bull feels, dying, gored by steel.

Chancy: All your lyricism, love speech, is dress
  For the nakedness of longing —
  Stark skin and sinews of loneliness,
  A roughness secreted in *Tulle*-laced songs,
  Prayers that dote to blasphemies,
  Whines masking the brute musk of fear.

Beatrice: Am I merchandise, so cheap to discount?

Chancy: Your plushest value is as merchandise.

The door gapes; lamplight worries the room.

Chancy: Quilt her till reds texture the floor.
  This April 3rd, this Good Friday,
  Let her feel my authority.

Dice: I'll handcraft lush, handsome lashings:
  Set blood and tears flyin like rain.

Beatrice: Your bone is my bone, your flesh is my flesh.

Chancy: Ply that cat's tongue again, I'll lop it off.

Exit Chancy.

Dice: Who you think you are, actin all mulish?
  You mangy, stubborn, dust-coloured bitch!

*Moonlight grates upon the graveyard. The wind is staggered by the
sounds of the whip — and worse — then resumes. The thin, biting
tone of E-flat clarinet insinuates bitter silences.*

Lustra sits in her chamber. There's a bandage near her mouth.
Easter Sunday.

Lustra: Mannishly, she intimates defiance—
    Mia dolce, Beatrice, sei afflita.
    Her eyes jig, tussle, unlovely with ire.

A knock! Lustra glides to the door and leads Beatrice into her
chamber.

Beatrice: (*Pointing to herself*) My body's an atlas of pain—
    Here's a Venice of tears, a Carthage of fire ...

Lustra: It's cold, so cold, so bone-gnawingly cold.
    And here it is April 5th, Easter.

Beatrice: How fares my love?

Lustra: The slave Lead breathes—even after fifty lashes.

Beatrice: This second-handed report destroys us.

Lustra: He moans in his cold, raw cabin.
    When Dice lavished salt water on his wounds,
    Lead howled enough to crack, break, burst, his ribs.

Beatrice: I fear that God hates sinners—
    All those who creep beneath His gaze.

Lustra: Then abandon Paradise, leave here now,
　　Blanketed by stars, if not your lover.
　　Unless you wife a gilded attorney,
　　Not some dull, base, brassy slave lacking coin.

Beatrice: Our worth's calculate: less than frippery.

Lustra: Bluntly, no joy is possible for you
　　Unless you bed some wealth bankers admire —
　　Or you vacate our Paradise for good.

Beatrice: Why shouldn't it be my father who flees?

Lustra: Remember, Bea, that your father made you.

Beatrice: Like he makes thieves and harlots of his slaves.

Lustra: To hear a woman speak thusly — so close to shame.

Beatrice: Would my words stab! I'm molested
　　By white men's words and black men's eyes,
　　Pawed by white women, and condemned
　　By my dark sisters' blunt talk, hard looks.
　　They pick me apart.

Lustra: For a piece of property, you quarrel much.

Beatrice: What's my crime? That I'm a woman?
　　And dark? My pains sue my mother's,
　　Who wrought her black flesh to white bone,
　　Whose sweat nourished, primed, these orchards,
　　Capitalized, flourished, on her pain.

Lustra: She was uncouth, unclean, unclad.
  And all her work was in my bed.

Beatrice: So jealous were you of her, you bolted,
  Shut her out, in raw, unpitying cold,
  Instigating a stabbing consumption.
  She spat up melting stuff when she perished.

Lustra: What was her business in my bed?
  A wife has rights. I was sick, sick,
  Of his slinking to her criminal flesh.
  I woke up, sobbing, shaking the dark,
  Heard him moaning over this nasty,
  Brindled sleeveen, this gargoyle quail,
  Sashaying in her loud rouge dress,
  Gabbling unkempt English. I felt her —
  Orange breeze — moaning moaning,
  Throning herself on his thighs,
  And I resolved to do what I did.
  I am still the mistress of this house.

Beatrice: At least she could beget. She was fertile.

Lustra: Your words heap burning cinders in my mouth.

Beatrice: I remember how she came
  To clasp me at night,
  After sweating all day,
  Sweating all day, in the fields,
  In the fields, my mother.
  I hardly learned to say
  Her name before she ...

Crying out her final breath,
Crying her final breath, crying.
I loved her.

Lustra: I loathed your mother — that nightmare rival —
But I was never able to love slavery —
All that flesh-fatiguing hatred. So, when
Your mother was failing, and asked I take
You for my own, I first begged Christ to fill
My vacant womb. He refrained. I divined
You were His blessing. I strove hard to hate,
But my heart refused; you became my child.

Beatrice: I'm still a slave; you've not suffered like me.

Lustra: This wound near my lips marks my love for you.

Beatrice: I never asked you to adopt my chains.

Lustra: Beatrice: My chains are invisible, silent;
But they weight me, they press me down.

Beatrice: Everything is weighted by love, I think,
And we often break.

Lustra: It's women's fate to endure
Dishonour, injury, pain.

Beatrice: Why?
Why should our tears be nectar
For *Sorrow*'s bees,

Who sting us with grief,
Metaphysical,
So skies burn black?

Peacock enters.

Peacock: Peace, I bring calming, consoling mercies!

Beatrice: Is *treachery* now a rhyme for *mercy*?
　　You news'd Chancy abruptly about Lead.

Peacock: I did what I thought right as your pastor:
　　Stay words that slash like accusing metal.

Beatrice: No, not metal: It's fire that's used against pus.

Peacock: I've a means to resuscitate *Justice*.

Beatrice: Since when have you cared a speck for justice?

Lustra: Beatrice, Peacock can gentle your father.

Beatrice: Hate's in him like a knife, cutting away his heart.

Lustra: Suffering should suffuse your faith, Beatrice.

Beatrice: Is my faith adequate?
　　I cringed in the cold bed,
　　Trying to hide. Loud air snapped.
　　Blood wept from his whip.

Peacock cracks a jetty, leather-bound ledger.

Peacock: (*Writing*) "A father who loathes his own flesh."
    Continue.

Luſtra: His guilt's inscribed in flesh.

Beatrice: A father who mounts to glory
    On our broken backs. Tancred-like.

Peacock: (*Writing*) "He diɛtates like God, judgmental and
    cross."

Luſtra: Perhaps not. He's handed Beatrice a poem
    Summoning her to Eaſter prayers this night.

Beatrice: He blasphemes, then calls me to chapel.

Peacock: Unfold his lyric, Bea, unfold his thoughts.

Beatrice: (*Reading*) "This morning is fiery Chriſtmas for me,
    Apple blossoms pink Eaſter-luſtrous air.
    Only you can love me to God, Beatrice.
    Every moment is a moment of becoming.
    Soft, in church, we'll softly confederate.
    Your love-besotted father, C."

Luſtra: Forgive him, Beatrice! Lure him back to God.
    You and I kneel often in the chapel.
    Go there sweetly, tonight. Nurture mercy.

Beatrice: I will go, but I require that Wentworth
　　Field troops to warranty my father's love.

Lustra: Beatrice, you forget your low place. Troops shield
　　White women. Peacock must act on my word.

Peacock: Depend on English religion, English justice,
　　Our English governor, Sir John Wentworth.

Beatrice: Hurry! *Love* trumpets charity for our degraded
　　　　beings!

Exit Beatrice and Lustra.

Peacock: A small lie here, a small lie there,
　　And truth is what I make it seem.
　　I'll wait, though it's *in extremis* to wait.
　　I'll go to Halifax — and do nothing.
　　Three weeks I'll linger there, three weeks,
　　Telling the governor nothing.

Exit Peacock.

❧

SCENE III

*Dreamt sunflowers crane towards a campfire. Yellow flares in
halted and suspended arcs. Dumas, Lead, Deal and Moses con-
spire, breathing words obscured by the quilts they have draped*

around their encampment. The stars lurk in darkness and crave digestion in eternity. Late Easter Sunday, April 5.

Dumas: His whip writes—fiery ink—across our backs.
Easter or no Easter. Our backs blister.

Lead: Dice whipped her just like you'd start up horses.

Deal: Her back's as raw as beef.

Moses: Let *Justice* crawl up out its hellish grave.

Deal: Their eyes hack ours—bone splinters and jelly.

Lead: We breathe pain, a kind of air,
As if we'd die without it.

Moses: We own nothin but our breath—
And Massa even poisons that.

Lead: Two-legged dogs come, pantin,
Smellin of piss and bad wine,
Sniffin up our mamas' dresses.

Moses: They serve hotcakes and whippings for breakfast.

Deal: Flay them up so bad their strokes would have strokes.

Lead: The moon swings back and forth—scythe-like.

Lead hammers a rock with a rock. This world is fire—it hurts, it hurts, it hurts.

Dumas: Purge, scourge, your heart with rum: that's
        the nice price
  For doing lousy nothing but breathing.

Deal: They take communion in the mornin;
  They take us to bed in the evenin.

Lead: With bitter steel, let's carve out a Heaven.

Moses: Heaven?

Deal: A world without white folk.

Moses: God, give us this day our daily bread.

Deal: Give us this day our lost children crushed like eggshells.

Lead: We are black — as coffee is black,
  Black — as earthy bread is black,
  Black and black and black.
  We mean beauty. Can I get an amen?

Dumas: Our dreams are frozen stiff and break apart.

Moses: Once there was a time we'd bow down to God.

Lead: When we bow down, our eyes blind with prayer,
  White men taste our daughters and our wives,
  Spreadin them in milkweed.

Moses: Why chastise God for men's satanic sins?

Deal: My innards was wrenched; ice gored my mouth.
   He used me like I was a mare.

Dumas: Who can contradict such malevolence
   Or stomach it?

Moses: Why doncha watch, wait, then scape with Beatrice?

Deal: You think she gonna step — free — out that house?
   You think Massa ever gonna let em wed?
   You think they can have any chillun here?

Moses: I heft a Bible to muscle my hands
   For eventual murders. My heart's iron.
   But I know: Vengeance be God's luxury.

Dumas: Let corpses slick downstream like logs,
   Christen the River Annapolis *Necropolis*.

Deal: These white maggots kiss us with pestilence.
   Their bright skins shine like lice.

Lead: Hear me, I'm sick — sick of whiteness:
   White pine white spruce white sheets white wine
   White lies whitewash white lightnin white
   Verse white sugar white meat white smoke
   White this white that. Let black *Death* troop!

Moses: Your speech be drastic, chilly and homely,
   So impoverished of any Easter joy.

Lead: Do we got any yelling cause for joy?
   What is this world but a dungeon of light?
   Naked as water, we's spewed from broken-
   Down thighs, to creep round this circuit of pain,
   And live as food for leeches, beetles, crows.

Moses: But ain't everyone meat for someone else?

Lead: I will have majesty! I will have it —
   My birthright! So what if pale monsters die?

The moon flaps cold. Exeunt all.

ༀ

*Chancy paces in a candle-wicked chapel. He sports his black hat.
Late Easter light.*

Chancy: I tempt my brain — or she lures me — to grave
   An organ in a fresh, unscabrous cleft,
   To be darkly traduced, a prize, vicious,
   Sap-eating triangle, housing noxious
   Buzzing of incestuous insects busy
   At sex, dumping blood — swank, nervous — like Christ's.
        Wantonly, I'll discover her verse —
   Wet, shining, under a black bush, a language
   That is flesh webbing us, the mouth feel of poetry,
   The Word in her mouth — like salt water,

Malicious, sad, like Clemence orchards
Torn apart by hail.
   Her flesh shall waſte into sin
Before it shall waſte.

Chancy metes out words like lumps of fire.

Chancy: Imagine a coſtly, well-kept diamond —
  Jumped, wriggling, cracked by a jeweller's chisel —
  A soft, ebony jewel, split tenderly,
  Then vomiting priceless ruby facets.

   My hands will speak horror to her body.
  She'll learn what it means to be property.

↜

SCENE V

The imago *of Jeanne d'Arc, or of Queen Makeda, B. kneels in prayer in a candle-wicked chapel. The Bible cannot easily be read in this darkness. Wearing a sleeveless French petticoat of albescent* faille *silk, with Chantilly lace flounces and embroidered scallops on a field of gold taffeta, and an opalescent bodice, B. soaks in the available radiance. Gold ropes her neck.*

The sound of tearing lace — or tears. Enter C., with F-minor music — note of immorality. He doffs his hat. The lampblack river ivories under ſtars. Later Eaſter night.

Chancy: (*Aside*) Beatricia, lovely Beatricia,
  As if in a Rubens,

Your lips halved to sing,
You pray, moaning—
Chaste voluptuousness.
              Your perfume on my face
Is like apples tumbled
In an autumn grove,
A place where *Poetry* comes to die.
I'll petition so lightly,
My words'll waken you like dew
Brushing grass at dawn.
              Oh God, if You do breathe ...
If You do judge!
Too late. All's resolved now.
(*To Beatrice*) Beatrice!

Beatrice: Father! I've answered your letter.

Chancy: Beatrice, you've satisfied my prayers.

Beatrice: I never thought you'd speak such loving words.

Chancy: I feel loved now that I'm here beside you.

*Outside, rain breathes around them like the holiness — or hollow-
ness — of the church. Across North Mountain, at Margaretsville,
the bay expires on minimal sand, without forgiveness. Wind-
stunned gulls hover, transfixed, fielding stiff and stiffening wind.*

Beatrice: God loves us, father. God adores sinners.

Chancy: Come, kiss your father Christian-like.

Beatrice: On the cheek, sir.

Chancy: On the lips, lamb.

Beatrice: I don't know—no, I don't—I can't.

Chancy: A Christian kiss beatifies us, Beatrice.

B. pecks C. purely on his cheek.

Chancy: I hate everything in this world but you.

Beatrice: I've also frowned upon this loveless world.

Chancy: (*Singing*) Flower o' the lute:
    Where love is not, there's only withered fruit.
    Flower o' the sun:
    I let her go, and all joy is gone.
    Flower o' the bell:
    I shan't weep, but a sunflower shall.

Beatrice: (*Singing*) The river's turmoil
    Issues cold, caustic brilliance,
    Whitening April.

Chancy: What means your parable, Beatrice, *stornellatrice?*

Beatrice: Over and over, we break rusted chains,
    Only to clasp to our twisted hearts,
    Fresher forms of the same old pains.

C. kisses B. on her lips.

Chancy: God, I want to love you more.

Beatrice: I already love you.

Chancy: You've no idea how much I mean.

Beatrice: Father, now we should kneel and pray.

As B. kneels, C. foams his face in her hair.

Chancy: Ahh, you smell of Heaven — of *crème-neige* or
opoponax.

B. jerks her head away, but C. yanks her against him by her hair.

Beatrice: I'm just meat, perfumed by its corruption.

Chancy: Your hair's dark perfume, pungent like sex,
That Jerusalem of orgasm, frames luscious
Sixteen-year-old munificence.
        I'll not wound that skin moister than felt,
That panics me with a sweetness like stars.
Your lips'll open up Heaven for me.

Beatrice: I am ... Please, stop. Innocent. Innocent!

Chancy: The sins of innocence are pitilessly damned.

Beatrice: What have I done? I was born — that's your fault.

Chancy: Your chastity, Eve, has a fault.

Beatrice: I've not wronged you. My heart is uncorrupt.

Chancy: Everything that comes puking
　　From between a woman's legs is corrupt.

Beatrice: O father, my life is as sweet as yours.

Chancy: Your lean thighs justify your mother's slavery.

C. slaps B. down on a pew.

Beatrice: Lead! Lead! O my sweet Lead!

Chancy: That boy lisps leaden syllables —
　　Yearning, yearning, yearning, yearning.
　　Instead, you feel your father's hands …

Beatrice: Have pity, father. Murder me instead.

Chancy: Half-black Negress, scented slave of *Nature*:
　　Easter demands such small sacrifices.

C. harries B., slits open her corset's eyes. Five scarlet lines lambaste his cheek.

Beatrice: No, stop. I'm your blood. This horrible blood.

Chancy: When you place a bit in a horse's mouth,
　　It also bleeds. It's natural. This blood.

Beatrice: Please, forget me, I am only spring grass.

Chancy: It hurts a bit, at first; some blood springs loose;
    But, after, there won't even be a scar.
    Béatrice, ma fille, j'ai envie de toi.
    Tu seras une avaleuse de foutre.

Beatrice: I hurt [*two words garbled*] my throat
    [*Several words whited out*] a knife.

When her father seizes her, B. cries like snow. Light slumps in darkness. When it returns, the chapel appears exactly as before, but deserted. Emotions linger — as if light were memory, a kind of excrement. Outside, stars bog down in mud — sorrow ground out of rain.

ACT IV: *REVOLT*

*She learns her lesson at once; to escape slavery
she must embrace tyranny.*

— CARTER

*Lustra's chambers. Beatrice enters, staggering, bedraggled. Lustra
shadows her.*

Beatrice: (*Wildly*) I was black, but comely. Don't glance
    Upon me: This flesh is crumbling
    Like proved lies. I'm perfumed, ruddied
    Carrion. Assassinated.
    Screams of mucking juncos scrawled
    Over the chapel and my nerves,
    A stickiness, as when he finished
    Maculating my thighs and dress.

    My eyes seep pus; I can't walk: the floors
    Are tizzy, dented by stout mauling.
    Suddenly, I would like poison.

    The flesh limps from my spine. My inlets crimp.
    Vultures flutter, ghastly, without meaning.
    I can see lice swarming the air.

Lustra: Your hair's a vulture's nest, Beatrice.
    Something's bruised and tattered your face.

Beatrice: His scythe went *shick shick shick* and slashed
    My flowers; they lay, murdered, in heaps.

Lustra: You cry like a broken Jerusalem.

Beatrice: My screams tumbled into my thighs,
There they gelled, coldly, to sewage.
There's wet snow burning, charring, inside me.

Lustra: These words bristle thorns: They savage and tear.

Beatrice: I'd gladly gash my neck,
Carve a collar of blood,
If I thought I could sleep.

*A violin mopes. Invisible shovelsful of dirt thud upon the scene —
as if those present were being buried alive — like ourselves.*

Beatrice: Did you spy God, lynched, dangling from a tree?

*Beatrice faints. Silenced now, the cannonade of the surf off
Clemenceport, this April 5.*

Lustra: Regard her face, raked with wet blush. Deal! Deal!

Enter Deal.

Lustra: Here's Beatrice, fallen.

Deal: Felled? Beatrice? The stars,
Sickly, couldn't bust with such rough damage.

Lustra: I fear some beast has whelped catastrophe.

Deal: A beast? Yes, no. A man's fathered these wounds.

The women settle Beatrice on a chaise longue.

Lustra: Boil milk and water! Bring iced water!
　　　Burn a fat pine and drop the dewing tar
　　　Onto scorched wool to tamp against her hurts.

Deal: It'll take more than that to doctor her pain.

Deal exits.

Lustra: Francis slurred to his bed, his eyes hissing,
　　　His fingers caucused with reeking trout,
　　　His pants fevered, his skin smirking
　　　With *crème-neige* and opoponax,
　　　And *cinq* scarlet scorings on one cheek …
　　　I fear what I must never dream.

Beatrice: (*Awakening*) Beatrice? What is she? Oh, Beatrice is
　　　　　dead.

Beatrice tugs at her hair.

Beatrice: His fingers infested my hair.
　　　Get me a knife: I'll hack it off.
　　　I want nothing on me that betrays me.

Lustra: Why do you tear at yourself?

Beatrice: His lungs coddling rats. His lacerating breath.
　　　He ransacked me. Flesh he made, then slit open. I —

Lustra: These words, Beatrice, gouge a grave in my heart.

Lustra comforts Beatrice. A crow lights heaven with the wick of its wing.

Beatrice: His thorny hair,
    His rabid hands,
    His ... his ... his ...
    Brawling in my corpse.

Deal returns, bearing a china teapot, a towel and a jug of cold water.

Lustra: Deal, smear some water on the cloth,
    Sop that vileness groping down her leg.

Beatrice smashes the water jug of Sèvres china. Addled rain chars the dark earth darker.

Deal: Chil! Chil! It's unhealthy not to clean this.

Beatrice: Don't give me water;
    I can't be cleansed!
    His stink's still on me.

Lustra: Let us wipe away — like tears — this battery.

Beatrice: It'll take a razor
    To disinfect the real filth —
    This obscenely worked skin.

Deal: She be cleft, clarted, clapped.

Lustra: Confiscated.

Beatrice: I knelt and prayed. He pried out my heart. I fell.
   He pushed. I feared God. He feared nothing. I wept.
   He jeered. I hurt. He enjoyed. I choked. He chafed.
   I groaned. He grinned. I was pure. He was powerful.

Lustra: She should be married; instead, she's martyred.

Beatrice: I hated the taste of his breath —
   An offence to my lungs.

Deal: (*Singing*) The sun burns us,
   The rain soaks us.
   Our bones wince in pain,
   But don't break;
   No, they don't break.

Beatrice: My womb's a fractured vase,
   Teeming, itching, with cockroaches.

Lustra: GodGodGod …

Beatrice: Ha! Don't utter that name.
   I want nothing more to do with Him.

Deal: (*Singing*) The dew chills us,
   The winds shake us.
   Our eyes cramp in pain,

But don't weep;
No, they don't weep.

Beatrice: My womb's a stew of vinegar and blood,
    Some Easter pollution.

Deal: Slaves no more than pigs are loved.

Lustra: O sweet Christ!

Beatrice: Sweet? By Lucifer, I'm sure he winked
    While someone stubbed twixt my legs,
    Pleasuring himself in my pain.
    His flesh ripped me raw like a whip.

Lustra: I look at you both and I am shaken,
    Set quite derelict in my marriage bed.

Beatrice: Sunlight be jagged and hurts
    Where it falls ...
    I'm black blackened blacker.
    Blood issues from thawing flesh, unsolid.

Deal: My eyes is destroyed. Her heart be destroyed.

Beatrice: If you do love me, snatch atrocious knives.

How can she forget that she was mired in candlelight, her malleable limbs traduced, that darkness hemorrhaged in her eyes, and that the culpable air, stucco'd with false stars, lithified her body while her fluids stanched the uncaring pew? There's no freedom this side of the grave.

Chancy's bedroom mirrors that in Titian's Venus d'Urbino. *The painting oversees the room. Saturnine oil lamps smudge the scene, damaging moonlight. Chancy bears a bandage on one cheek.*

Chancy: Know there's shame still smutting the pew
Where she collapsed under me, too the musk
Of her body like massacred lilies,
Unsacred flowers.

Chancy dallies on the bed.

Chancy: I can still hear her sigh, "Please, father, please,"
Like some nesting, unsated tease,
Making this Easter what she had to have.
I wager she enjoys this joyous sin.
            I'm inebriate of paternity,
Like Lot, and my girl's come into my cave.

Lust animates a Hell from dust.

Chancy: I'll go pell-mell between her thighs,
Netting take after take of nectar
From a malfeasant dankness.
I'll ride her a-cock-horse hotly,
My hands pious upon her breasts.
She'll mutter, "Oh oh oh oh oh!"
Over and over again; her *belle* purse
Odiously alive and screaming
For more and more pleasure.

It'll nullify all virtue.

I'll beget son and grandson,
While she gets son and brother.

~

Beatrice sits on the floor of a barren room. Lucina *glints above cold
pines.*

Beatrice: The body shivering in silk,
    The body broken in two.

He rode me — a sweating horse,
    Whimpering, panting, gasping.

He frothed, toxic, moiling
    In the disgusting pew.

I've died here in just four days,
    But won't be resurrected.

Beatrice stumbles to the window. Her face sheens in a phthisic gloom.

Beatrice: Dragooned, suddled, temerated —
    I'm out-and-out his drawbreech now.

His eyes writhe lice-like upon me.
    I am impure. I am unclean.

He pestled me against the dismayed pew,
Raped my dress so the eyes juped:
Roaches rattling the floor; his breath gnashed.
After, I wiped blood from the pew.

Dovunque io vada,
L'aure per me diventan tosco.

He's crafted a world where words must sound
Steel skirmishing with steel.

Easter concludes with the whispering of knives. Stars, at last
exhausted, wink out.

༉

SCENE IV

The garden. Slaves, sunflowers, stars, sparks. Quilts strung on trees
muffle speech. Lead conspires over rum. Nisan 25, or Sunday, April 19.

Deal: He stuck his ramrod down her clean muzzle
    Two Sundays ago, and he's still breathin.

Lead: Massacre every piece of his pale hide!

Deal: His eyes spittled and tore down her clothings.

Lead: Damn, he's not goin to have any eyes left.

Moses: Ain't nothin of men's hands lasts in God's eyes.

Deal: Why's it always the hated who must love?

Dumas: In white churches, they soil the bread,
　　Turn wine to piss, and shit on us
　　As we toss in beds of torn gospels.

Deal: The gospel be the view between our legs.

Moses: We gotta love folks into the Kingdom of God.

Deal: While white men knock us into Hell.

Lead: What's wrong with you, Moses? You used to be
　　Hebrew-like, violent, not some stupid,
　　New-Testamented, half-demented priest.

Deal: Too flowery, backboneless, weak-brained, mushy.

Dumas: Moses was once sly; now he's just silly.

Moses: Jesus counsels me not to counter Chance.

Deal: You talkin like you been fuckin Lustra,
　　Like, if you pile enough sugar on shit,
　　It'll start to look and smell like chocolate cake.

Lead: We need a bold, black Moses, not some yellow Christ.

Moses: I'll listen to God! Y'all do what you like.

Lead: I'll slash his shocked face with leeching gashes;
　　Laugh, and wipe my drooling blade on his sucking lips.

Dumas: Abominate his abominable
    Flesh with nasty, gulping hemorrhages.

Deal: Bash his outsides in, chop his insides out.

Moses: Fix your eyes on the dove!

Dumas: Doves, doves, are burning. They char white
        and drop.

Moses: The Bible drips with myrrh.

Dumas: It sops with blood.

Deal: That book's only good for provin how white folks lie.

Lead: I ain't gonna be lead no mo. I'll lead.

Lead smashes the rum bottle against a rock and selects a shard of glass. His shirt weeps apart. His found blade scrapes away a cruciform brand. Sunflowers burn the night.

Moses: Christ took spikes through His palms to redeem us.

Lead: My howls'll hammer Heaven and spike at God!

Dumas: Loving black smoke and black currants,
    Loving blackbirds and black-eyed Susans,
    Loving black sheep and black whisky,
    Loving black rum and black pepper,
    Loving blackest night and black women,

Loving black black and blackish black,
Loving ... Death grows clearer, clearer.

Lead howls and throws away the glass.

Lead: I'll plough the orchard with ſteel murder, pluck
  Down greasy corpses crabbing apple trees.

Deal: There's never salvation without a death.

Moses: Chancy's life be our doom.

Lead: His death be our freedom!

Exit all but Deal.

Deal: I'm gonna get myself free. Get myself free. Uh huh!
  In the tousled bush, I'll guttle blackberries, wild cherries,
  and hazelnuts. I'll jig eel and rig me fresh eel pie. I'll gulp
  dandelion coffee after dicin up the roots, roaſtin em in a
  hardscrabble ſtone-oven, then ſtirrin the duſt into boilin
  water in the pot I'll liberate to cover wages owed. I'll eat
  bee pollen and ſtrawberry leaves and blueberries from
  burnt-over acres. I'll mix a decoſtion of milk and daisies,
  the meal of daylily, the morning's dew, and a smidgen of
  clover. The wind'll fix my banquet. I'll slog out in the
  damp, bed down in bogs, take rocks for my pillow, and
  willingly suffer smelly, hot fens, mosquito swamps,
  and agues and fevers. I'll venture every hidden space of
  a well-hidden road. When I come out the woods, I'll
  lap rainwater from my sore palms. I expeſt it'll hold the
  sugar taſte of freedom.

＊

SCENE V

The library. Chancy hunkers in a cave of books. He swills annihila-
ting rum. Dice shivers into the room. Outside, brush strokes of rain
watercolour the heavens, a clear Turner, as a woman drifts, weeping,
through Paradise. Orchard country. Tuesday, April 21.

Dice: *Hatred*'s kindlin the air.
    These are cautious days, sire;
    Not for the incautious.
    I've sniffed out a knife, sleek,
    Cocked inside Deal's pillow.
    She swore it's for her nails!

Chancy: Rope'll chafe their skinny necks —
    Pimping, meeching creatures.
    They'll not redden my groves
    With nigger-engendered death.

Dice: I hate Lead's fierce, pitchforkish looks.
    Lemme dice him like so much pork.

Chancy: Wentworth will dispatch seven
    Agreeable soldiers
    Who'll smooth whipped-up waters.
            Until their horses come,
    Batten Lead hard in his cabin.
    In a fortnight, I'll ship
    His hide from *Paradis* to Mississip.

Dice: Whacha gon do bout the high-yellah gal?

Chancy: Beatrice? She's going to kill me.

Dice: (*Laughing*) She *that* good?

Chancy: Fool, you wrench my stomach. What if Beatrice
    Were part your sister? Would you love me still?

Dice: Ain't you my papa? Ain't you called me forth?

Chancy: You're good as a son. No more I'll say. Go!

Dice jumbles out. Chancy gulps a cat's-head-pint of white rum.

Chancy: Her lips fall sour, gall, with separation.
    They'll not be kissed, glad, into submission.
    Like Dante's Beatrice, she's devoured my heart.

Enter Moses.

Moses: Massa, Miz Lustra call me to serve you.

Chancy: Moses, why do I vomit the Bible
    Verses you mouth and tongue with relish?

Moses: Massa's gotta make Jesus's flesh his meal;
    Massa's gotta drink only Jesus's blood.

Chancy: Prayer crimsons itself in my throat and mouth;
    It bloodies imagination. I feel
    Immedicable stabbings rouge my throat.

Moses: Massa, you've worshipped the wrong god too long.

Chancy: Dirt clogs my Bible. It puffs filth. Leave me.

Exit Moses.

Chancy: Her sourly usurpèd sweetness,
    Her bitterly surrendered honey …
    Her pain is juſt like love.
        God, why did You mandate a man
    Who loves to plunge in his own flesh?
    I've worked out my own damnation.
        Harrying a niche, a lozenge of flesh,
    I am sepulchred in my own flesh—
    A self-ample cemetery.

Chancy swigs some rum.

Chancy: God, God, this cataſtrophic air is duſt;
    The ſtars are foul, burning shit.
    What have I done?

He sits up, downs more rum.

Chancy: God, ulcer her skin, so I can sleep,
    Not be driven to that plush couch,
    To juxx, to rutch, *futuo* …

    I wake up hearing the ugly
    Sucking noise of our love—
    Leeches on a wound.

    There's nothing more. I'm at an end.

My soul's laid aside from sickness.
I've violated faith inviolate.

Lustra enters. Her bouquet of roses is a quiver of arrows.

Lustra: I bring roses, love-coloured, from our pleasance ...

Chancy: These flowers gangle tawdry, mongrel,
    Bad-tempered, their pouting crimson
    Snatches foaming slugs—
    Gleamings of guttural poems
    Amid dark loves, forbidden—
    Opera, sufficing no one.

    They smell like false women
    Come from diseased gardens.

Lustra: My lord, my love, let me nurse you.

Chancy: You see, she cuts me with her eyes—
    Eyes as incinerating as teeth.

Lustra: Savour your wife: My body's Puritan.

Chancy: My eye slices women into commodities.

Lustra: You obscure the whole point of love.

Chancy: This hot thing below your waist's the source of evil.

Lustra: My lord, it's only God-designed nature.

Chancy: *Nature* is a gross machine of eating and fucking.
　　The air we breathe comes from inside a pig.

Lustra: You've drunk too much, I think, that's all.

Chancy: (*Wildly*) While Father crisscrossed seas for slaves,
　　Mother uncrossed her legs for slaves.
　　She shaped perspiring vermin: damned,
　　Gross, panting things. Are you not damned?

Lustra: Women are always blamed for men's sins.

Chancy: I knew my mother. She was a harlot.

Lustra: And the men she knew, what were they?

Chancy: Eunuchs.

Lustra: You have a brain fever; sleep, sleep.

Chancy: The heavens come apart like virtue—
　　Or a pair of legs—breachable.

Lustra: Why don't we abandon this flowery waste,
　　Become new loves kissing wine in exiles' cabins?

Chancy: A man knows death before he feels it:
　　He swears and drinks too much of abomination;
　　He giddies to bed, feeling cold, the cold of sheets,
　　The cold of moonlight executing his neck,

The cold of the woman beside him;
His love turned to ice, gelling his heart.

Lustra: You frighten me, my husband.

Chancy: You don't understand. Understand me now.
She's poisoned the stones of the earth gainst me
While crows splinter in mid-air and drop.

Note her capital, decapitating look,
The steel, sharp, of a hardness that won't bend;
That body like unloving steel. Dirty.

The bricks have gone deaf since she ceased to sing.
Things rot that once were flowers, horses, nuns.
I've dribbled lye into an alcove of honey.

Lustra: Oh my husband, you romanticize sin.

Chancy: I stare at her, shake. When will God slay me?

Lustra: Slaying? Why this palaver on slaying?

Chancy: I hate anything that breathes. Death is just.

Lustra: Too soon, worms blast our flesh to bits. Too soon.

Chancy: Hand me Hawk's book on slitting deer.
Splay the malicious diagrams,
Charting ways to insult a throat,

With callous thrusts of a rude blade,
Till blood shoots in spurts, not volumes.
But I'll not puncture guiltless deer.

Lustra: These words render black wolves that rend my heart.

Chancy: I'm felled by women. I mean fish merchants.
Light hurls dark glances at us. I love her.

Two weeks since I slaughtered her, I love her.
Mark her thank you and her farewell of hair.

Chancy faints. Rum leafs and sprouts from the bottle. Lustra gazes abstractedly upon her spouse. Outside, the night's agog with rain. Oceans unravel in the pines. Anyone suffering calenture would drown easily in the Annapolis River—the jittering, irritated river.

Beatrice, in black velvet, appears at the library entrance, hunkers in gloom.

Beatrice: (*Aside*) God, that I were a man and had a knife,
I'd gouge out his heart, firk out his eyes,
Anatomize his stomach—
Ce Jefferson provincial,
Who appalls and hectors me
With a jellied bone,
Who knows no qualm of love.

Beatrice enters the room and signals to Lustra to join her on the other side, near a fireplace.

Beatrice: Is he dead?

Lustra: He's quaffed too much and collapsed — like a flooded
        bridge.

Beatrice: If he were dead, he'd sleep better.

Lustra: Hush! He's your father!

Beatrice: Call him as you like. I call him my raper.

Lustra: These words aren't poetry, Beatrice: They canker.

Beatrice: You like poetry, so here's sweetheart poetry:
   He wants me for his piece of brown sugar,
   And he wants you to watch him licking it.

Lustra: These *faisandé* words reek of death itself.

Beatrice: He'll not stud me until I calf bastards —
   Nor continue scarfing sluts in your sheets.

Lustra: You observe him viciously — like a wolf
   In the short silence
   Between itself and the deer.

Beatrice: Must I again shiver under him,
       Going cold,
   Bear his jagged incesting,
       As if loving it?

Lustra: I'm not myself, but a stranger,
   Blundering in shadows.

Beatrice: I should cut him and cut him and cut him
　　In his eyes, throat, lungs, heart, stomach, no end …
　　For sixteen days I've suffered. He can die.

Lustra: I look at you and I eye a gallows.

Beatrice: Stop pretending holiness:
　　We haven't got it in us anywhere!

Beatrice snatches a Bible from a table.

Beatrice: Is this the Bible I gave you?

Lustra: The same.

Beatrice: It's made of wasps' paper that wants burning.

Beatrice thrusts the Bible into the smouldering fireplace.

Beatrice: No more white lies, no more black pain.

Lustra: That's a tragical performance, Beatrice.
　　But save it for theatre, not real life.

Beatrice: How hard, pure and cold language —
　　Like war or love — must be!

Chancy groans, snorts, turns, slow as a beached whale, in his sleep.

Beatrice: I could sign his death warrant in a breath.

Lustra: Is his thin breath such an insult to God?

Beatrice: You brain ill cats, smashing them against walls.
     This killing's no different.

Lustra: How can you stipulate this and live?

Beatrice: Fuse his rose tea with laudanum. He'll drowse.
     Then ... abolish him with a stroke.

Lustra: Murder's unforgiveable, Beatrice.

Beatrice: To destroy love,
     That's the only
            Unforgiveable sin.

Beatrice rages out. Winds prune the earth.

Lustra: Once this man loved me. I remember:
     He'd seem gigantic, falling over me,
     A look scribing his face like peace.

Lustra strokes Chancy's face, a mask afflicted with a living rigor
mortis.

Lustra: But pain cores me now. He's slain me from within.

     Too many lies and mistaken things and vexing things.
     Too many lost things and doomed things and crippled things.

     Love lays between us like a cemetery.

❧

Moses, carrying a Bible, encounters Beatrice in the garden. April 21.

Moses: Bee, neglect of Jesus wounds to damnation,
    And your contagious rage scares the meek from God.

Beatrice: You must be a Baptist, Moses, a rundown one.
    Your eyes are narrow as a Baptist's thighs.

Moses: You'll get true strength by leanin on God's Word.

Beatrice: Old man, your strength's just got too old —
    True strength isn't cobbled from surrender.

Moses: Hold fast to God: He's hidden midst His stars!

Beatrice: I put no faith in stars. Our killers are
    Massed assassins who outnumber the stars.

Exit Beatrice.

❧

SCENE VII

The Governor's office. Province House, Halifax. Gullsquawks and seamurmurs filter through the crimson drapes of Sir John Wentworth, a refugee from tyrannical America. The Loyalist rules a maple desk. Peacock preens before him. Friday, April 24.

Wentworth: I have ugly news from Marie Uguay —
　　　Who's down in Nictaux trying to grow grapes:
　　　(*Reading*) "Francesco Cènci, of Paradiso,
　　　Was viewed scuffling with, and scrunching behind,
　　　His own daughter, Biétrix, who was weeping."
　　　I know Chancy. I fear this note's imply.

Peacock: (*Shrugging*) Your Excellency, Governor Wentworth,
　　　In Nova Scotia, lying is an art.

Wentworth: This tale — if honest — is unnatural.

Peacock: If honest, he's done what is natural;
　　　A song as old as rain; he has chopped wood;
　　　He has tilled a field; it is nullity.
　　　Will clouds die, stand still, become fixed things?
　　　Men keep but the ruins of the Bible.

Wentworth: I have a carriage-sent letter, dated
　　　Tuesday, April 21st — three days past —
　　　Where Chancy warns of an insurrection
　　　Apprehended among his apple fields.

Peacock: Because you've sired a colley named Colley,
　　　That is — pardon me, sire — a black bastard,
　　　Off some Jamaican Maroon sable mare,
　　　Planters fear you'll sire emancipation.

Wentworth: The Planters have no cause to grouse. They spawn,
　　　Like Chance, mulatto litters of their own.
　　　Censure Ochterlony's *seraglio*!

What about Haliburton? Is he chaste?
Bah! Nova Scotians do nothing but drink—
And rut. Their legislators just vomit.

Peacock: Slavery is perishing anyway, Sir John.

Wentworth: At ice pace. Peacock, go to Paradise,
    Quell any disorder, refresh the peace,
    Defile F. Chancy to the capital,
    In the sovereign name of George III.

I'll instruct my officers of your equipage.

Wentworth exits. Alone, Peacock opens a cabinet, withdraws a bottle, sniffs its contents, then pours it into a tall glass, which he drains.

Peacock: Sly as Dante's seraphically dark houri—
    Sloe-violent, Gioconda eyes,
    Sable hair ivying carnal gold.
    How she'll slender at touching things ...
            I have a dream of her mauve lips moaning,
    An idea of evil moisture,
    Avoirdupois hot as the *Inferno*'s tercets.
    She makes me see flesh, so I hunger.

I'll be ensconced in her soft grave—
Christ!—before I'm tumbled in mine.

A second glass ...

Peacock: Love is the root and trunk and branch of all evil
    And invention in this constantly rotting world.

The history of passion is littered with lying bodies.

Sometimes too much to drink is not enough.

꒰

A sunrise breaking stars. April 27. Beatrice, garbed in black, wanders in the cemetery.

Beatrice: Will you trudge through lightning?
   Will you let the city damage my poor?
   Will you smash down the door to take me?
   Will you suck my breasts till they're raw?
   Will you bury me in unfrugal rain?
   Will you heal me of white grammar?
   Will you salve my busted eye and stubbed heart?
   Will you lick my cat till it gleams?
   Will you do this and do that?
   Will you come inside my garden and come again?

   My persecutors are God-breaking machines —
   Ravenous, albino, indecent.

   How long must I feel a knife at my throat?

From the azure middle distance, Dice regards Beatrice warily as she exits.

Dice: Crazy, yelluh quail. She intakes some cock,
   And she squawks off half-cocked. She ain't my sis.

And I don't trust her addled act one part:
She'd squeeze a perfume outta shit itself.

A wrinkle of electricity — lightning revelling in the eye, then the pear tree blackened by fierce, quick rain. The stream is shouting torrents. All theories of beauty heap up corpses.

SCENE IX

Lead's hut. Still Monday, April 27. A pitch-pine lamp crackles, affixes its beam. Blather of keys, jangle of a bolt.

Lead: Who be there?

The door yields. Lead, in woollen pantaloons and ankle-chains, spies Chancy in a gold-trimmed black cloak and a broad, shadowing hat. Near-homicidal shock.

Beatrice: (*A hushed blurting*) It's me — Bee!

The hat falls; mahogany hair falls. Lead tenses, relaxes. Beatrice bends to unlock his chains.

Beatrice: I shaped myself demonically
   To slip, unpursued, my prison,
   His nunnery of pain,
   For Deal spirited me a key
   To havoc the lock on your cell.
   It dangles, compromised.

Lead tries to embrace Beatrice. She undoes his ankle-chains, slips away like a mirage.

Lead: I loves you terribly, poor belover.
    These past three weeks my eyes be agony
    Not seein you. Your daddy's kept you jailed.

Beatrice: My lover's my father: When he broke me,
    He was like … it was like crows tearing meat.

Lead: I feel myself becoming sharpened metal.

Beatrice: When he treads nights into my room,
    The air sinks, sullied, into grease
    Intussuscepted by my throat.

Lead: I'll end him!

Beatrice: I breathe his corruption by breathing air,
    Astonishing my lungs with posh poison.

Lead: I swear, I swear I'll …

Lead stretches forth his hand. Beatrice grants him a silver dagger. He holds it like a crucifix.

Beatrice: His blasphemed chapel sheltered this relic.

Lead: Here's the one cross I'll worship, this weapon.

Beatrice: Tomorrow's moon, don't let him wake alive.
    Twist this key in his throat; his breath will out.

Lead: A small gash is enough to destroy him.

Shrieks.

Beatrice: What was that?

Lead: Nothin.

Beatrice: Banshee horses
    Whinnying and hashing the earth.

Lead: I don't hear nothin.

Beatrice: They're eating each other alive …

Lead: Haps it's the sea — smashin this world to bits!

Beatrice: That night, he sacked all that I'd saved for you.

Lead: Stabbing him will be like forking manure.

Beatrice: Slouch his corpse in orchard branches,
    Make it feel like he fell and was skewered.
    We must be better killers than lovers.

Lead: He'll feel the pain I felt scraping his brand.

Lead shows Beatrice his wound. They sit on his rude bed. Rain riots, smashes, ululates. The lamplight stares down the storm. The not-muscular, yet-heroic light.

Beatrice: In a dream, I cut Christ: He bled a sewer.

Lead: I loves you as close as frost on apples,
    I dream I hold you like holdin a river.

Beatrice: We must hate before we can love.

Lead: April'll blow rain and snow pon us;
    When we sprawl, free, in an open field,
    That ocean yellin at our feet.

Beatrice: April's almost gone; April's finished.
    I was dreaming, dreaming too much,
    As if love could extinguish history.

Lead: Your lips're like half-open flowers …

Beatrice: Don't kiss em; they're carnivorous.

Lightning cannibalizes night. Beatrice remembers Jeremiah 8:21.

Beatrice: (*Singing*) "For the hurt of the daughter
    Of my people am I hurt; I am black …"

*Lead buckles Beatrice — modern Ruth — to his scarred chest.
Above the storming cumulus clouds, a star-angry night wheels,
cursing the world with flinty light.*

Beatrice: (*Murmuring*) The blue moon shadows
    Silences of black water,
    My love like a delicate flower.

He curls, vivid, violet,
In the nest of a poem,
Its dark love, its shadows.

Pines, breath, eyelashes, wind.

After the rain, Beatrice's head is encircled by the sumptuous moon, suckled against a cluster of yellow stars. She becomes Tituba.

SCENE X — INTERMEZZO

The garden. Moses and Dumas mourn under the April moon. One guitar's a weary heart.

Moses: Can't move no stone
    To let my saviour out.
    Can't move no stone
    To let my saviour out.

Dumas: Can't move your heart
    If I start to doubt.
    Can't move no stone
    If you won't help.

Moses: Can't find no love,
    Gotta find my Lord first.
    Can't find no love,
    Gotta find my Lord first.

Dumas: Can't get your love:

I damn well must be cursed!
Can't find no love;
Things can't get no worse.

Moses: Can't drink no wine
   Without my saviour's bread.
   Can't drink no wine
   Without my saviour's bread.

Dumas: Can't make no love
   Without her in my bed.
   Can't drink no wine;
   Might as well be dead.

*The deep stormy moon — a pearl against Nubian ebony — swanks
into the night.*

Moses: That poem hurts me — like singeing rain.

Moses exits. Does the ocean wash in, flaming?

Dumas: The blue sigh of murder cankers the breeze.

*A dark-haired girl sits, dark-eyed, by a white lamp. She shakes,
once or twice, her dark hair by the pale lamp.*

*Dumas: L'ombre de la lune bleue,
   Sur les silences de l'eau noire:
   Mon amoureux est une fleur délicate.*

*Il s'enroule, vif, violet,
   Dans le nid d'un poème —*

Son amour sombre, son ombre.

Pins, souffle, cils, vent.

A cloud blots the moon. Blossoms moan.

Dumas: Is death the death of love?

Petals are fallen against the rosewood grass, a few others are crest-fallen amid thorns.

Dumas: (*Singing*) *Il neige sur l'Acadie*
    Comme il neige dans mon coeur.

Strumming sadly while watching the moon.

Dumas: A drowned man floats
       Face down
       In a jet-black sea.

Three stupendous, unseasonable sunflowers, one huge as a jack-o-lantern, mottle the moon. The river, ivre, *unravels rain.*

Dumas: (*Singing*) Come into life in skin and bones,
    Hold some lover to make you whole.
    But when you die, you lie alone:
    Melt to bone in a cold, black hole.

Dumas degresses from Marot to Metastasio, scaling from bel canto *to tragedy, accompanied — in memory — by a harmonization of* fagot, flageolet, ophicleide, violin piccolo *and* zink. *Then, a liquid blackness suffocates light. Monday, April 27, finishing.*

Faut-il assassiner le tyran?

— TRUDEAU

SCENE I

Conspirators loiter in the library. Beatrice is draped in black. Note the magnesium colour of the leaves and the sombre fioritura *of the church bells, bawling in the tempest.*

Lustra: He was so, so, tender tonight
When we undressed, sweetly tender.
I almost fell in love again …

Beatrice: Where were your tears when he was tearing me?

Lead enters; his dagger tosses lightning. Tuesday, April 28. A whole moon.

Beatrice: Demonstrate you're forged of sternest metal.
Dismantle sick organs, demolish sick eyes.

The lovers kiss. A wild diaphony of violins and chimes.

Lead: Let me murder everything white.

Beatrice: We'll kiss and kill and kiss again,
Feeling only pleasure.

Lead: His death will come—like I snap my fingers.

They kiss again. Lead exits.

Lustra: My lord kissed his cross at supper;
I sense he wants to turn to God.

GEORGE ELLIOTT CLARKE

Beatrice: If you hadn't wanted him to perish,
　　　　You shouldn't have grovelled to be the one
　　　　To serve rum and opium-tincted tea.

Lustra: Husbands and wives share mysteries of forgiveness
　　　　I wouldn't expect you to understand.
　　　　That laudanum was a wife's last gift to her husband.

Beatrice: Hear that? A sou'wester shatters and howls.
　　　　Four weeks ago, returning, I heard that.

Lustra: One blow cancels a father and a husband.

Beatrice: He you describe is nothing to me.
　　　　The Gospel of Love is tore up.

Lustra: You've concocted poison and treachery.

Beatrice: To ask for love and be given lye,
　　　　To ask for freedom and be given wounds:
　　　　That is poison; *that* is treachery.

Lustra: We can still rescue love, if we have faith.

Beatrice: That was a lustrous faith I once trusted—
　　　　Pain ulcered—an abortion—in my guts.

*Lead returns. On the Minas Basin, a beach shines with water later
to be ice.*

Beatrice: I feel—Huh? Done quickly? Finished cleanly?
　　　　Is he dead? Stymied? Exterminated?

Lead: (*Shaking his head*) My fist hunkered to strike ...
   He hollered, "Cripes! Cripes!" in his dreams.
   I figured he'd fuss, slobber blood on me.

Beatrice: My anger is like hunger: Satisfy it!

Lustra: A sign! Don't assassinate him!

Beatrice: Bitch!

Slap! Lustra falls, weeping. The sky scowls over the sea, breakers seething home.

Beatrice: Slave days is over!

Beatrice seizes the dagger from Lead's fingers.

Beatrice: Must it always be women who slaughter
   Hateful, recidivist, two-leggèd beasts?

Lead grabs Beatrice; she slams him in the face with the knife handle.

Beatrice: You play at murder as if in a play.

Lead: We'll butcher him into one yelling wound.
   His blood'll baptize, smother, our four dark hands.

Sfumato *waves scroll along a beach.*

Lustra: His blood gluts your veins, but you crave it on your
   hands.

Beatrice: My dagger's ice; it numbs any feeling.

Beatrice leads Lead towards the door. She can no longer distinguish desire from disease. They exit.

Lustra picks up a gleaming silver letter opener, fondles it.

Lustra: Cold weather's gelled
    With constant rain.
    Death freezes in my brain,
    Like hysteria, fruitless —
    A white, broken music,
    Unutterable.

Gripping the letter opener, Lustra touches herself, remembering.

Lustra: This black evening's full of dark shapes and
            things.
    Are stars hurling themselves against windows?

    The great stride upon vast and infirm
    Nothingness. Rain blows down like a pall.

A scream. Lustra drops the letter opener and paces the room. Lightning — a lynchee — twists.

Lustra: When we first married, he'd descant
    Some words spat out, others suffocated,
    Some words, nervous, choked at articulation:
    (*Singing*) "No poet singing love, his head thrown back, am I.
    I creep no roads to yell at stars;
    I've prayed, but only rain has fallen, only rain.

When will you fall?" *Et cetera.*
We swilled harsh wine and slept in grass.

Lustra licenses a soliloquy. The sound of love dying.

Lustra: I was eyeing daffodils when I discovered
    I loved you, that Easter, straying from church.
    You were white innocence, your breath making
    Love to air, your beauty distressing eyes.
          We fell to intoxicated grass.
    I held a half-eaten plum I let you finish.
    I fell deeper into the perfumed grass:
    I was slender, and it was your pasture.
          Too soon, we forgot kisses that drove us
    Into the grass so hard that stars fell.
    You leaned away, away, cut from me,
    A river seething white in its bed.
          My blood mimics that river now,
    A pain like ice lurking, titanic, within.

Unseen, Chancy's body sprawls, shocked — like the subject of David's Marat assassiné.

Lustra: Well, well, well, well, well, well, well.
    Snow mounts and mounts and amounts to nothing.

Enter Beatrice and Lead, red-spattered, raked by light — astounded by their capacity for cruelty.

Beatrice: I hacked his alabaster face in half.

Lead: Like bilge, the monster's ill breath gushed away.

Beatrice: Fluid gucked out, hot, drooling like flies.

Lustra: My brain's hurt; my heart bursts; my hands are to
   blame.

Beatrice: His death leaves stars unmoved in space.

Lead: Encunted, the dagger fucked his left eye.

Beatrice: I've never felt freer. This rain glints gold.

Lustra: You act like a Charlotte Corday, one ripe in tint.

Beatrice: Then serve me red wine! I'm ravenously happy.

*Lustra nears Beatrice and stares at the scarleted dagger. She pulls
from it a few hints of hair.*

Lustra: Is my spouse this — just gusts of hair?

Beatrice: If I could, I'd obliterate
   Him — every iota —
   Pelt, feces, meat ...

Lustra: Where's my lord?

Lead: We drizzled rum in his throat, tarred his breath,
   Posed him like he'd dropped, from his balcony,
   Skunk-drunk, and got gouged by apple-tree limbs.

Lustra: My husband—he lies out there—barbed in a tree.

Lustra weeps. Beatrice slaps her lustily.

Beatrice: Shut up! He lied to you, then lied on me.

Lead: He'll no more gallop his whip cross our backs.

Beatrice and Lead sound a deep kiss.

Lustra: (*Laughing, crying*) Look at you—the daughter of her
         father!

Beatrice: Guiltless, my gilt hand was his guillotine.

Lead: His pig blood—on your hands—smells all rosy.

Lustra: So God help me! You are a crude killer,
   Who used slaves' small griefs to license great crime.

Lead: I had the right! I was the slave! It was
   His turn to feel the gutting pain he served.

Beatrice: Rapacious, he had a rapacious end.

Lustra: You murder and talk and act innocent
   As mild water that drowns struggling infants.

Beatrice: (*Shaking Lustra*) Why should a man's death mean
   Any more than the death of a fish?
   At least we can eat a fish.
   Don't cry over spilled blood.

Lustra: (*Wincing*) These April stars are vile infanticides:
 What is the use of our breathing?

Beatrice points her stained dagger at Lustra.

Beatrice: Ply that cat's tongue again, I'll lop it off.

Lead: Let's cut her neck and chuck her down there too.

Lustra: Chancy's dying breath has dyed your hearts black.

Lead menaces Lustra, but Beatrice clasps his hand.

Beatrice: Lead, creep back to your cabin, drowse.
 If anyone interrogates the sheets,
 I'll claim that slushy queans encrimsoned them.
 Not for the first time ...

Lead and Beatrice kiss again.

Beatrice: We'll found ourselves a Canaan of perfumes.

Lead: I've never loved you more. Never more loved.

Lead exits. Lustra whimpers.

Lustra: Stones, splinters, sticks, scissors, spikes, stirrups, scythes.
 A Bible? No Bible. We're going to die.

Beatrice comforts Lustra.

Beatrice: We're free, Lustra. We'll live no more like beasts.

We'll eat cornbread, gulp wine, and drink
As much light as our eyes can hold.

Lustra: He was an honest man, more or less.

Beatrice: A violent man, with the morals of a tumour.

Lustra: I'm hunted — like a timber wolf — to death.

Beatrice: Come, cheer up, and help me to wash,
From my hands and clothes, this gored blush.

Dumb show: Beatrice begins to disrobe as Lustra pours water into a basin. Beatrice scours her face and hands with a cloth, then shifts behind a screen to change her dress — from black to white. Lustra collects the incriminating tissues and places them in a covered vase.

Beatrice: His blood's like dirt: It scums off in water.

Lustra: Can water rinse away murder so easily?

Beatrice: Why not? It seems to work with rape.

Deal: (*Singing offstage*) Steal away, steal away, steal away to
Jesus.
Steal away, steal away home:
I ain't got long to stay here.

Thunder, cannon, hooves. Further surges of rain.

Lustra: Why are the slaves singing?
Some evil has happened.

Beatrice: We'll live, free, by Lawrencetown Beach—
　　Where heaped waves—constant moaning silk,
　　Cleanse light, wash and freshen it,
　　So the word *Love* pours itself forth as ocean.

Shouts. Shots. Thunder. Hurried steps approach, Beatrice seizes the dagger and tucks it inside her gown. A breathing alarum, Deal pants into the room.

Deal: Dice be draggin Chance, slashed up, smashed,
　　From a busted-up apple tree.

Beatrice: What?

Deal: The rough storm damages.
　　Look t'yo'selves.
　　Troops troop.

Deal exits.

Lustra: Why did you have to stab a snoring, drugged old
　　　　　　man?

Beatrice: Do you want to hang? Pusillanimous dreamer!

Lustra cries. Beatrice cradles her stepmother's head against her breasts. Thunder, cannon, hooves. New steps. Moses enters.

Moses: The mouth of the Church Road
　　Is blocked up with white men.

Moses exits.

Lustra: My love's hung in a tree; we'll hang from one.

Beatrice: Peacock swoops, slavering, with soldiers. Too late.
   It's April 28: He's three weeks late.

Lustra: What is worse than drama is clarity.

Beatrice: Be lawyerly, cold-eyed, and we will sing.

Enter Dumas.

Dumas: What is death? History. What is new?
   His blue eyes lie sprawling upon his cheeks.

Exit Dumas.

Lustra: (*Laughing harshly*) Torches! Light! A vinegary light!
   Something to clean up this darkness ...

Beatrice: Learn to thrust your fear deep under the dirt.

*Angry rain. The downcome dirges. Beyond this trauma, the river,
cast forth from its gorges, spurs an apocalyptic flood.*

*A flourish of drums and African-tuned bagpipes. Martial steps.
Peacock enters, latches to Beatrice's side. Two Royal Nova Scotia
Regiment soldiers, clad in red jackets with royal blue facings, grey
trousers and regimental colours, post guard. One brandishes the
Nova Scotian standard. Dumas, Deal, Lead and Moses congregate
just inside the door.*

Peacock: Gentle ladies, I came as soon as God allowed.

Moses: Justice is sweetest when soonest.

Lustra: You're too late. He's dead. My love was mortal.

Beatrice solaces Lustra by soothing her teary face with her hair.

Dumas: He fell like autumn,
   His brain springing dreams.

Dice enters. He possesses the cunning of the endangered.

Beatrice: Tree limbs stabbed, capriciously, my father.

Moses: He fell — like all sinners.

Deal: How black the dark. How bolted down the moon.

Dice: One apple tree dangled weird fruit on it.
   It were his system, all broke up:
   Limbs doubled up, squashed and splintered.
   My only father, destroyed like waste fruit.

Lustra: Dice, how can you claim his paternity?

Dice: I knows it like I knows you cut his breath.

Peacock: This act of God ...

Dice: My father slotted her (*points to Beatrice*) and slutted her
         (*points to Lustra*).
   I wager his death is their act, not God's.

Beatrice: His charges stink of lynching. His lungs lie.

Lustra: How could anyone dream we'd harm Chancy?

Peacock: Though bleak, this tragedy is natural.

Dice: There's no wood bits in his eyeholes. That says
  Devils — these fierce women — dashed out his eyes.

Peacock: I'll judge if anyone has trespassed here.

Dice: (*Pointing at Beatrice and Lead*) They be lovers —
  This hussy and her lucifer.

Lead: You dog-faced liar! Ain't you just like a dog?

Lustra: Does no one hear the psalms of innocence?

Dice: These cold bitches and their pimp lies so hard,
  They could crumble mountains into pebbles.

Peacock: Custody them so we custody truth.

A soldier moves towards Beatrice and Lustra.

Lead: I'll trash and bash your face, Dice. Just get close.

Dumas: (*Aside*) This goes freakish. We'd best scape while
    we can.

Deal: (*Aside*) White man's justice does evil. Time to scat.

Moses: (*Aside*) Since Chancy's dead, let's just go like we're free.

Beatrice: Arrest us, and you arrest the truth.

Dice seizes a bayonet from a guard and rushes at Lead.

Dice: Lead's the butcher who fatted this slaughter.

Dice gluts the bayonet in Lead's back.

Peacock: Order!

Beatrice aims her dagger through Dice. He falls. Battered, the vase of bloody clothes shatters.

Lustra: Dying is hard; murder makes it harder.

Peacock: These ruddy cloths cry incrimination.

Dice: Bitch! Blood of a bitch! Beat rice! Bloody, rotten bitch!

Beatrice: I pray your death tastes like acid to you
  Because it's like honey to me.

Dice dies.

Peacock: Guard the assassins! And clear this congregation.

One soldier guards Beatrice and Lustra; the other moves to clear the room.

Deal: My Lord's gonna rain down fire

One of these days, hallelujah!
And if He don't, I will.

Self-freed slaves exit.

Lustra: I'll weep these green years when I should be gay.

Beatrice: Lead!

*Lead coughs, choking. Beatrice cradles his head on her lap. Garnets
trickle onto her gown.*

Beatrice: Lead, Lead,
　　Your blood is fragile rubies.
　　If I had to annihilate this world —
　　This womb of horrors —
　　To let *Love* live, to let you live,
　　I'd do it.

Lead: (*Singing*) Black pearl.
　　You're a dark
　　Black pearl …

Lead dies. Chivalric, beautiful failure. Beatrice weeps.

Beatrice: I caress your going, a soft letting go,
　　A torn breath,
　　Dark words hinting of strawberries.

　　Air will taste different without you —
　　A brine of thorns.
　　A crush of words marshalls to your name:

Earth — baked, kneaded, pounded into bread.
Earth — packed, squeezed, and pressed into wine.
Lead.

Darkness shatters and falls on the valley.

Peacock nears Beatrice. A medley of asides ensues.

Peacock: I could have saved you. I would have spared you.

Beatrice: Why? To play your pliant and grateful whore?

Peacock: You should be more elastic, less like iron.

Beatrice: Knowing what they know about human nature,
 I don't know why pastors don't commit suicide.

*Peacock exits. A soldier prods Beatrice and Lustra to the exit. This
time, in dreams, is one of slain horses.*

Hubbub. Commotion. Darkness. Hammering, Sawing.

꙲

SCENE II

*Beatrice is in black in a black cell. Monday, October 5. To conceive
of her inquisitors, think of swine.*

Beatrice: (*Monotone*) I pinned a viper's eye to something that
 hurt.
 His blood gusted across my palm.

I ſtuck a coffin smack in his neck.
   Consider that I was never free,
Never safe from an invoice of shame,
My heart cracked open and there was only extinĉtion.
   That night, fusillades of rain smashed French horns,
That night, horses whickered in the murk,
That night, five months paſt, I was deadly as a church.
   I'd rubbed raw the New Teſtament, weeping,
The Old Teſtament, praying. I cut him
Two gashes, and he bled like a butcher.
   White men, you took away my freedom
And gave me religion.
So be it: I became a devout killer.

ᵏ

SCENE III

Zebra shades. Moonlight. Luſtra doʒes on her seaweed-woven palette as Beatrice meanders in their cell. Our Lady wears a black dress over petticoats. Thanksgiving. Monday, Oĉtober 12.

Beatrice: My life's a prison that *Death* will unlock.
 Like Marie-Josèphe Angélique,
 Like Évangéline Bellefontaine,
 I'll suffer what I muſt.

There'll be no blossom on the branch, no tides washing the face or breaſt, no salvific kiss, no cotton wedding dress, no chorus from the *Song of Songs*, no love on the bones, no tenderness, no escape.

I should remember only love.
One white night I laid awake in your arms,
Watching the moon powder your naked skin.
I cried all night to hold you in my arms
Because this was my dream. I loved you,
I love you.

A cell door clangs. Crows howl. Skeletal men trundle a cart heaped with skulls to market.

Beatrice: I remember Dante now, the violence
   Necessary to pry open Heaven:
   Io venni in luogo d'ogni luce muto.

The powdered moon chafes mauve through the dying indigo and the massed branches. Wind lays waste to the last of summer, buffeting birches to distil leaves.

Beatrice: Rain and autumn waters commingle,
   Bejewel trees and me,
   Wind in the beautiful,
   Ruined trees awaiting new beauty,
   And wind in this wracked body,
   Also to spring new beauty,
   Fresh and refreshing love.

Unspoiled, the wind among the alders. Lustra awakes, groggily.

Lustra: A coffin is being shut around all light.

Beatrice: Hush, Lustra. We must bear witness to light.

Lustra: I was not a flower for this age.
   I twined myself around a fatal tree.

Beatrice: Our childbirth is sinning and pain:
   We make love by the sweat of our brows.

Lustra: Our Paradise has gone to hell.

Beatrice turns to the window. The gallows sprouts like a fatal weed.

Beatrice: Looking towards Nictaux,
   In the scudding dusking,

   Scent of ripe, rain-wet apples—
   Sharp like apple blossoms—

   I find it hard to breathe
   Outside of poetry.

   I near death:

   I can feel blood pushing
   Behind my eyes.

Lustra: Is *Death* our Thanksgiving, our lustration?

Beatrice: It's so easy to die, so difficult to love.

Lustra feels Beatrice's five-months-pregnant abdomen.

Lustra: Is this Lead's child — or my husband's bastard?

Beatrice: This innocent is blessed:
It'll not breathe our infected air.

Lustra: Is death the price of happiness?

Beatrice: One cannot enter the New Jerusalem
From the prison-house of breath.

Beatrice begins to caress Lustra's face and hair. Lustra, weeping quietly, responds in kind.

Beatrice: This morning, we'll stroll
Through autumn blossoms,
A morning gushing leaves
And last breath-taking petals.

A scirocco curls through me.
The dark blue awakens, the stars slumber.
We'll not wake again to such leaves.

All we were will vanish
Like October flowers.

J'oscille doucement comme les feuilles
Affligées par le devil.

The landscape is transfigured by unfulfilled love — every leaf, twig, and runnel is stamped by its impression. A faint smear of light; then, the dawn surges through the lushest quarter of the pines.

Hubbub. Glooming. A brain-matter-coloured sky. A gallows in the Paradise village triangle. Peacock, in a black-hooded robe, roosts atop the scaffold. Guards lead Lustra and Beatrice, bound, both in black, with long silk shawls over their heads, to the scaffold stairs. Sad drum. Muffled fife. Leaves pamphlet the square. A violet bell bleeds in the white wind. The soon-dead ascend to the summit. The wind is furious steel amid still-drooping, frost-charred sunflowers and, now, damaging snow. Beatrice regards the audience and, briefly, lowers her eyes—in the manner of Vermandero. For Thanksgiving. Savage, martial piano. Hungry paupers assemble with bejewelled plutocrats—Lycanthropi—while Peacock tenders his speech.

Peacock: Good folk of Clemence,
   Justice yet survives.
   Paradise shall not
   Shelter parricides.

   Francis Chancy was
   Cruelly slain unsaved.
   Governor Wentworth
   Has freed Chancy's slaves.

   Thus, Lustra Chancy
   And Beatrice Chancy
   Will float by their throats
   Until God they see.

Beatrice: (*Aside*) God, save me from this world of weak light
   And misgivings: Shatter this penitentiary of flesh.

Lustra: Non mi piace il Paradiso.

Muted trumpet, piano, drum. Enter a rump mob of Planters, drunk, huzzaing, firing rifles, leading whinging dogs from dishevelled villages. Two commence a game of cards at the foot of the scaffold; another sucks wine from a sack.

Deal: My God! — to hang a pregnant woman,
    And on Thanksgiving, as if it were war.

Moses: Let those who've not sinned be those who hang our folk.

Dumas: We move in a punishing constellation.

Beatrice: (Aside) The globe contracts
    To the O of a noose.
    I'll waste, becoming words.

Lustra: (Aside) Every bit of evil on earth
    Has found its way to us.

Dumas: Precious in the sight of the Lord,
    Viatrix, is the death of His saints.

Deal: (Singing) I'm chasin the moon, chasin the moon,
    No more auction block for me.
    Moonlight's branchin through the trees,
    Many thousand gone.

Lustra: (Aside) This rope gnawing my throat is white wolves'
        teeth,
    Serrating my soft flesh, biting it thin.

Deal: Gone — the horse of a whip cracking my back.

Moses: Who will bother to write her Bible?

Dumas: I'll compose her Bible. Implacably,
   She thrust David's knife in Goliath's eye.

Deal: If they drove spikes through her palms, honey would
   ooze out.

Dumas: Annihilate her and you nullify
 Seven millennia of poetry.

Peacock: (*Aside*) The extra weight in her belly'll hang her
   straight.

Nooses — like necklaces of blossoms — garland the necks of the condemned. Peacock fidgets. A hacket-coach limps along tramp-beaten roads, slouches home through accidental snow dark with stars. The corduroy road tamps the swamp. Pictures are hung, people are hanged.

Lustra: (*Shrieking*) Have mercy! Oh, but you men have no
   hearts!
 Botched, debauched, you are malignant things!

Beatrice: Don't weep! We'll seize Paradise today.

Beatrice graces the scaffold. Atlantic-wounded, Blakesque faces moon over her martyrdom, this méchanceté. Her text is the cry of a woman who has come at last to the end of herself.

Beatrice: Sunlight burns inside the clouds. Look! They glow!
    Nous vivrons dans une idée de la liberté.

Hangman: I'm a poet, though a hangman by trade,
    But I've no happiness in this business.

Beatrice: Be of good cheer: My name means happiness.

Hangman: What can I do to afford you comfort?

Beatrice: Rapture my throat.

Hangman: It will rupture. Please, what more can I do?

Beatrice: Lay us down under ſtars so thick,
    We breathe fresh grass and shout in tongues.

Luſtra: I'm blameless! Don't injure me! I'm breathing!
    O men! I don't bleed daintily: A scratch —
    And I juſt fountain blood. Lend me mercy.

Beatrice: (*To All*) I bring you fresh, blushing apple blossoms—
    They waft the perfume of liberty.
    I bring you pale, fragile apple blossoms.
    It took violence to cut you these flowers.

Liberateds: Glory! — Oh yes! Yes — sweet glory!

Beatrice: Luſtra, my ſterling Lead, I'll keep *Love*'s sun
    Steeped in our tombs in endless Thanksgiving.
    It's all but all.

Drumrolls. A cannon peals. Light wails, bruised, peeling. A meringue storm pitches the Atlantic.

Liberateds: (*Singing*) Oh freedom, oh freedom,
   Oh freedom over me.
   And before I'd be a slave,
   I'd be buried in my grave,
   And go home to my Lord and be free.

Mind the extended ⁶⁄₄ chord in which Beatrice hangs, the dissonant second G, subtly cohering with the first F-sharp, a hymn of death. The globe goes dark as crucifixion times, light garbed in sackcloth and black ash. Ita n'è Beatrice in l'alto cielo.

When Lustra is hanged, she plummets two yards, jerks. She suffers a shock-like seizure, a pressing pain that gnashes her jaws so tightly, she can feel the nerves in her face and in her teeth. Then, her neck ligaments rip apart, separating the bones in her spinal column. Red leaps from her mouth. Lips rhyming laughter *and* slaughter.

Yet later, when believers strip Beatrice from her noose, they find no mark upon her skin. ("A few allow Death to touch them and leave / No scars or broken bones or longing.") Yet, chunks of precious flesh have been torn, wholesale, from Lustra's face.

Because this drama has concluded, we cannot see the women veil Beatrice's face for burial. We can imagine, however, her sepia cadaver, lapped in ivory muslin, interred in the maremma near Blomidon, not far from where ... Évangéline Bellefontaine wept while burning at the stake. Nowadays, liquified diamonds can be found, with diligent combing, at the marshy site — the Nova Scotian Camargue — enshrining Beatrice's remains. Not long a

drive to La Plage Évangéline with a good horse. Mark her
calendar date: 7e Floréal.

The wind seeds exculpatory, lily snow over the everfresh green of
the pines. On the Minas Delta, the Fundy surges, almost pitching
October's brimming tides over the grieving Acadian dykes. Then
the downy, falling down downfall of dark, dusty snow.

Fin.

£34 Reward

Runaway from the Subscriber, on the 16th Oct. ult., his negro boy GEORGE, aged about 43 years. He has a gothic-ugly countenance, is lye-tongued, but peddles plausible lies; he is a tan-complected African, coppered with Micmac blood, has a watery build, with tide-long arms, rain-long fingers, and a scar, serpentine, rippling down the back of one hand; the toe next to his great toe was split open by a ho'; his moony spectacles are bent crooked; he affects a black felt beret, half worn, but is not French, though he yammers off a nastily embastardized Acadian. He stands about five feet & ten inches, weighs about one hundred and eighty pounds. He has a remarkably high forehead, but likes to keep his eyes half-closed. He walks fast, and talks and laughs loud. He yacks a cursed, saltwater yinkyank, and fancies himself a poet, but is handier with a razor. Think him a threat. Like a Haitian Jacobin.

The sworn funds will be paid on his cartage to me, or to any gaol in lush, judicious Nova Scotia. All who hide or hire the said, I promise, will be pitilessly prosecuted.

GOD SAVE THE KING!

DR. JOHN BUCHANAN-
SAVAGE, ESQ.
Physician & Attorney
Wolfville, Hall County,
Nov. 1, 1801

*

*Noises of panting, running, muskets, creaking
hounds, snarling wheels, sagging wind, moon scream-
ing in the trees, the Gaspereau River groaning.*

— JUNIUS

*

Apologies

A story Friday should have said that the popular form of arthritis is osteoarthritis, not rigor mortis. *The Gazette* apologizes to our literate readers.

A second story Friday chastised Etna MHA Pierangelo Raphael for calling Annapolis Royal MHA Exalaphat Hart a "mild & broken-in Lothario." In truth, Mr. Raphael called Mr. Hart a "mildewed and broken-down harlot." *The Gazette* deplores such impolitic language.

A third story Friday claimed that Sore Rose (or Eros Sore) was hanged last Tuesday for stealing seven loaves of bread. Actually, she was hanged for stealing a jug of Thanksgiving wine. *The Gazette* pledges to correct every wrong.

CONVICTION

Las Beatrices producen amores incommensurables.

— SKÀRMATA

This work moves in sympathy with many visions of the true but often altered story of Beatrice Cènci, beheaded at the age of twenty for the crime of parricide, on September 11, 1599, in Rome, Italy. My echo shadows the dramas by Vincenzio Pieracci (1816), Percy Bysshe Shelley (1819), Juliusz Slowacki (1843), Walter Landor (1851), Antonin Artaud (1935) and Alberto Moravia (1958); the romances by Francesco Guerrazzi (1854), Henri Pierangeli (1933), Philip Lindsay (1940), Frederic Prokosch (1955) and Susanne Kircher (1976); the chronicles by Stendhal (1839), Mary Shelley (1839), Alexandre Dumas, père (1839–1840), Robert Browning (1864), Charles Swinburne (1883), Corrado Ricci (1923), Sir Lionel Cuſt (1929), Kurt Pfiſter (1946) and Irene Mitchell (1991); the film/screenplay by Bertrand Tavernier and Colo O'Hagan (1988); the parody by Kathy Acker (1993); the sculpture by Harriet Hosmer (1857); the photograph by Julia Ward Cameron (1866); and the operas by Guido Pannain (1942), Berthold Goldschmidt (1951, 1995) and Havergal Brian (1962). These creators have dallied with Beatrice Cènci, but I have committed indiscretions.

Too, I have admired the Beatrices found in Dante Alighieri's *La Vita Nuova* (1292–93); Giovanni Boccaccio's *Decameron* (1348–53); William Shakespeare's comedy, *Much Ado About Nothing* (1600); Thomas Middleton's tragedy, *The Changeling* (1653); Alban Butler's *Lives of the Saints* (1756–59); Vincenzo Bellini's tragic opera, *Beatrice di Tenda* (1833); Heſtor Berlioz's *opéra-comique, Béatrice et Bénédiſt*

(1862); Dante Rosetti's painting, *Beata Beatrice* (1864–70); Anonymous's erotic sweet, *Beatrice* (ca. 1900); Charles Singleton's *Essay on the Vita Nuova* (1949); Gérard Mourgue's lyric suite, *Amour de Béatrice* (1966); Max Pécas's blue film, *Les Mille et un perversions de Félicia* (1975), Antonio Skàrmeta's novel, *Ardiente Paciencia* (1985); Robert Harrison's study, *The Body of Beatrice* (1988); Beatrice Cenci's sculpture retrospective, *Beatrice Cenci* (1981); Isabella Vay's *récit*, "Beatrice" (1994); William Strickland's documentary, *Malcolm X: Make It Plain* (1994); the Beatrice Restaurant at 1885 Oak Bay Avenue, Victoria, British Columbia (1995–1996); and The Beatrice Restaurant at 268 Corso Italia, Ottawa, Ontario (1992–1997).

George Bourne's *Slavery Illustrated in Its Effects upon Women and Domestic Society* (1837), Benjamin Drew's *The Refugee* (1856), Harriet Jacobs's *Incidents in the Life of a Slave Girl* (1861), Carrie Best's *That Lonesome Road* (1977), James Oakes's *The Ruling Race* (1982), and James Mellon's *Bullwhip Days* (1988) yielded historical ana. John Fraser's *Violence in the Arts* (1974) ordained the act titles. Esther Wright's *Blomidon Rose* (1957) purveyed sweetmeats of geography. Lewis Poteet's *The Second South Shore Phrase Book* (1985) plotted diction. Benito Mussolini's *The Cardinal's Mistress* (1928) and Elly Danica's *Don't: A Woman's Word* (1988) incited insights. Robert Cooperman's *In the Household of Percy Bysshe Shelley* (1993) was a pure model. Jaime Augusto Shelley and Ann Plato were presiding spirits.

Close readers served to execute this work: Sandra Barry, Barry Cahill, Chan Wai See, Preston Chase, Boyd Warren Chubbs, Elizabeth Cox, Paula Danckert, Arnold Davidson (1936–99), Kwame Dawes, John Fraser, Marwan Hassan, Emiko Morita, David Odhiambo, Simone Poirier-Bures, Silvia Ross, Evelyn Shockley and Daniel Wideman. James Rolfe, Colin Taylor and Choucri Paul Zemokhol shocked it into being. Heather Sangster made it beautiful. Lynn Henry gave it intellectual coherence and style. Michelle Benjamin liked the story from the first time she heard it, late one night, over the phone in 1993. Val Speidel set it — gracefully — in shimmering Fournier type with elegant sienna highlights. Many thanks to Sherman Hines for permission to reproduce his historic map of Nova Scotia. Geeta Paray-Clarke and John Crawford found calendars for 1801. All the tragedy's infelicities and immoralities are wholly mine.

Merci to the Canada Council for a politic grant and to the Ontario Arts Council for an impolitic one. Thanks also to the Music Theatre Department, The Banff Centre for the Arts, for a grant assisting the completion of the first draft of the libretto version. Special thanks also to the Rockefeller Foundation for granting me a month's stay at the paradisal Villa Serbelloni in Bellagio, Italy, and to the McGill Institute for the Study of Canada for allowing me a term off to complete this project.

Beatrice Chancy was crafted in Ottawa, Durham, Arles and Bellagio, between 1993 and 1998.

INFERNO: STAGE PRODUCTIONS

Cientos de voces desencajadas por la ráfaga.

— SHELLEY

FOUR SCENES FROM *BEATRICE CHANCY* WERE PRESENTED AT
THE VANCOUVER PRESS CLUB, VANCOUVER, BRITISH COLUMBIA,
ON NOVEMBER 19, 1995.

Original Cast:

Beatrice	Celeste Insell
Chancy/Lead	Author
Lustra	Emiko Morita

A DRAMATIC READING OF *BEATRICE CHANCY* TRANSPIRED AT
THEATRE PASSE MURAILLE, TORONTO, ONTARIO,
ON JULY 10 & 11, 1997.

Original Cast:

Beatrice	Sonhia Dillon
Chancy	Graham Harley
Lustra	Donna Goodhand
Rev. Peacock	Victor Ertmanis
Fr. Moses	David Collins
Lead	Philip Akin
Deal	Camille James-Adams
Dice	D. Garnett-Harding
Dumas	Shafiq
Hangman/Wentworth	Roger Honeywell
Director	Colin Taylor
Producer	Leslie Lester
Stage Manager	Naomi Campbell

Co-Producers, Canadian Artists Network —
Black Artists In Action & Theatre Passe Muraille

ACT ONE OF THE OPERA DEBUTED AT THE CANADIAN OPERA
COMPANY, TORONTO, ONTARIO, ON JUNE 7, 1996.

Original Cast:

Beatrice	Christina Clark, soprano
Chancy/Lead	Doug MacNaughton, baritone
Lustra/Deal	Measha Gosman, soprano
Fr. Moses	Peter Wiens, bass

Musicians:

Dave Carlisle, Percussion
John Hess, Piano

Music by James Rolfe
Produced by Queen of Puddings Music Theatre Company
Conducted by Dairine Ni Mheadhra

THE COMPLETE OPERA WAS WORKSHOPPED AT THE MUSIC
GALLERY, TORONTO, ONTARIO, ON DECEMBER 15, 1997.

Original Cast:

Beatrice	Measha Gosman, soprano
Chancy	Gregory Dahl, baritone
Lustra	Lori Klassen, soprano
Lead	Vanya Abrahams, baritone
Deal	Lisa Lindo, soprano
Fr. Moses	Marcus Nance, bass

Musicians:

John Hess, Piano
Rick Sacks, Percussion

Music by James Rolfe
Produced by Queen of Puddings Music Theatre Company
Directed by Michael Cavanagh
Conducted by Dairine Ni Mheadhra

THE OPERA PREMIERED AT THE MUSIC GALLERY,
TORONTO, ONTARIO, JUNE 18–20, 1998.

Original Cast:

Beatrice	Measha Gosman, soprano
Chancy	Gregory Dahl, baritone
Lustra	Lori Klassen, soprano
Lead	Nigel Smith, baritone
Deal	Lisa Lindo, soprano
Fr. Moses	Marcus Nance, bass

Musicians:

Mark Fewer, Violin
John Hess, Piano
Sharon Massey, Double Bass
Richard Sacks, Percussion

Music by James Rolfe
Produced by Queen of Puddings Music Theatre Company
Directed by Michael Cavanagh
Music Direction by Dairine Ni Mheadhra and John Hess
Set and Costume Design by Jerrard and Diana Smith
Lighting Design by Paul Mathiesen

COLOPHON

And if the African belief is true, then somewhere here
with us, in the very air we breathe, all that whipping
and chaining and raping and starving and branding
and maiming and castrating and lynching and
murdering — all of it — is still going on.

—BRADLEY

Beatrice Chancy was designed and typeset by Val Speidel in 11 point Monotype Fournier on 13 point leading. Fournier typeface is the masterpiece of its creator, the Parisian type founder Pierre-Simon Fournier (1712–68). Blending classical and modern designs, it fuses elegance and clarity. Arguably, its italic face is the most exquisite in all of typography. Cover and interior photographs are by Ricardo Scipio. Printed on 55lb. Hi-Bulk Cream paper by Friesens in Altona, Manitoba, for Polestar Book Publishers, *Beatrice Chancy* has come through exile.

GEORGE ELLIOTT CLARKE was born in Windsor, Nova Scotia, in 1960. He has published three books of poetry, including *Saltwater Spirituals and Deeper Blues* (Pottersfield, 1983), *Lush Dreams, Blue Exile* (Pottersfield, 1994) and the acclaimed *Whylah Falls* (Polestar, 1990), which won the Archibald Lampman Award (1991). He is the editor of three anthologies, including *Eyeing the North Star: Directions in African-Canadian Literature* (McClelland and Stewart, 1997). He is also the author of an opera libretto, "Beatrice Chancy" (1998), with music by James Rolfe; a feature-film screenplay, *One Heart Broken Into Song* (1999), directed by Clement Virgo; and another verse-play, *Whylah Falls: The Play* (1999). Revered as a poet, Clarke's honours include a Bellagio Center Residency, awarded by the Rockefeller Foundation (1998), and the prestigious Portia White Prize, awarded by the Nova Scotia Arts Council (1998). Clarke taught African-American and Canadian literature at Duke University (1994–99), served as the visiting Seagram's Chair in Canadian Studies at McGill University (1998–99) and currently teaches world literature in English at the University of Toronto.

BRIGHT LIGHTS FROM POLESTAR

Polestar takes pride in creating books that enrich our understanding of the world, and in introducing discriminating readers to exciting writers. These independent voices illuminate our history, stretch the imagination and engage our sympathies.

Poetry:

WHYLAH FALLS *by George Elliott Clarke*
Clarke writes from the heart of Nova Scotia's Black community. Winner of the Archibald Lampman Award for poetry.
0-919591-57-4 $14.95 CAN/$12.95 USA

I KNEW TWO METIS WOMEN *by Gregory Scofield*
Stunning in their range and honesty, these poems about Scofield's mother and aunt are a rich, multi-voice tribute to a generation of First Nations people.
0-896095-96-8 $16.95 CAN/$14.95 USA

INWARD TO THE BONES: GEORGIA O'KEEFFE'S JOURNEY WITH EMILY CARR *by Kate Braid*
In 1930, Emily Carr met Georgia O'Keeffe at an exhibition in New York. Inspired by this meeting, poet Kate Braid describes what might have happened afterwards.
1-896095-40-2 $16.95 CAN/$13.95 USA

Fiction:

DISS/ED BANDED NATION *by David Nandi Odhiambo*
"Thoroughly convincing in its evocation of young, rebellious, impoverished urban lives ... an immersion into a simmering stew of racial and cultural identities..." —*The Globe and Mail*
1-896095-26-7 $16.95 CAN/$13.95 USA

POOL-HOPPING AND OTHER STORIES *by Anne Fleming*
Witty and engaging stories by a superb new writer. "Fleming's evenhanded, sharp-eyed and often hilarious narratives traverse the frenzied chaos of urban life with ease and precision."
—*The Georgia Straight*
1-896095-18-6 $16.95 CAN/$13.95 USA

WEST BY NORTHWEST: BRITISH COLUMBIA SHORT STORIES *edited by David Stouck and Myler Wilkinson*
A brilliant collection of short fiction that celebrates the unique landscape and literary culture of BC. Includes stories by Bill Reid, Ethel Wilson, Emily Carr, Wayson Choy, George Bowering, Evelyn Lau, Shani Mootoo and others.
1-896095-41-0 $18.95 CAN/$16.95 USA